The Mystery of

Rascal Pratt

by Robbie Scott

[signature: Robbie Scott]

illustrations by Gary Cianciarulo

Greenwich Mill Publishing

Mount Pleasant, South Carolina

For information on how to obtain additional copies of this book, contact:

Greenwich Mill Publishing
P.O. Box 1978
Mount Pleasant, SC 29464

Cover design by Gary Cianciarulo

Manufactured in the United States of America by the
J.R. Rowell Printing Company, Inc.
Charleston, South Carolina

ISBN 978-1-60402-519-4

Printed in the United States of America

For my mother, Patricia

Contents

The Mystery of Rascal Pratt

- 1 -

The Ends of the Earth

*The 29ᵗʰ of March, 1866: 1 frigate, the Gamma, flying British colors, 1 three-masted schooner, 2 fishing yawls, 1 brigantine bound for Peru.**

Emma Green copied these words into her journal. She copied them from her father's log and then folded her journal shut. Her journal was a small black book with a leather cover her mother had bought for her in San Francisco. It wasn't as big as her father's log, which was also a journal of sorts. When his log was open, it covered the whole desk, and when Emma closed it, the entire desk went *THUMP!* But when Emma closed her journal, it hardly made any sound at all. So she opened her journal again and shut it harder. This time it closed with a little thump, and a few specks of dust flew up off the desk and into the air. That's better, she thought.

Emma was twelve years old. She wasn't particularly tall, but she wasn't small either. She had brown hair, which she almost always wore in two braids, one behind each ear. There was nothing out of the ordinary about her appearance, though occasionally her brown eyes glimmered with a certain, arresting twinkle. Some people said the twinkle was

---

*Frigate, schooner, yawl, brigantine, all types of sailing vessels. A vessel is the fancy word for ship. A frigate is generally a warship with several masts and a gun deck. A schooner is a sailing ship whose rear mast is the tallest. A yawl has two masts and the front one is taller. And a brigantine is a two-masted schooner, whose front sail is the older, square kind, like you've seen on pirate boats. In fact, brigantines were originally used by pirates! *(A note from the journal of Emma Green – E.G.)*

willfulness, others said independence. But of course Emma could never see it herself – it was always gone by the time she got to a mirror. So she never knew exactly which it was, willfulness or independence. On this evening though, far from her old home in Rhode Island, and in this strange, new place, it could not possibly have been either.

She had arrived in California only a few days before, very excited to be moving to the shining, new city of San Francisco. But now here she was, just a few days later, stuck in a lonely outpost, practically the wilderness, where it seemed as though almost everything outdoors was dangerous – and ready and waiting to get her. At least, this is what everyone seemed to want her to believe.

For example, if she got hurt (or so she was told), she would probably be so far from anywhere she would die before help ever arrived. If she got in a boat (or so she was told), she would probably be swept out over the horizon before anyone ever saw her sail. If she so much as put her toe in the water down at the beach on the far side of her father's lighthouse, a wave would probably come rushing up, knock her over, and roll her down into deep water – and even if she didn't drown, her parents would never find her and she'd be dead in forty minutes anyway on account of the cold. These were the sorts of things people seemed to want her to believe and, whether they were true or not, they certainly kept her indoors.

It hadn't started that way. Four days before, her brown eyes probably *were* brimming with willfulness – or independence or whatever it was – but also, and especially, they would have been brimming over with adventure. For after a hundred days at sea – more than *three months!* – the ship on which she and her mother and father were passengers had finally sailed out of the vastness of the Pacific Ocean and glided into the glistening waters of San Francisco Bay. On that evening, excitement crackled in the air and all the passengers crowded the rail to watch as the ship drew closer and closer to the city. Even the sailors, whom Emma might have imagined had seen everything there was to see and could never be excited by a thing so routine as coming to port, scampered about the decks like boys, adding even more sail, as the great clipper ship skimmed from crest to crest over the last few miles of its journey.

Emma's family was coming to be lighthouse keepers. This made them a little different from the other passengers. Without exception, everyone else aboard the ship with whom Emma had spoken over the last three months – and that was probably everyone – seemed to be coming to California for the exact same purpose: to get rich. Gold, silver, land – it was all to be had in California, everyone told her, and if you didn't walk away rich in a year's time, then you probably were a fool. Lighthouse keeping seemed rather plain in comparison. In truth, though, this suited Emma just fine. She was glad to already have a purpose in this new land.

Emma was the daughter and only child of John Green, *Captain* John Green. Not too long before, he had been an officer in the U.S. Navy. He had even been a hero in the Civil War. Emma was enormously proud of this, even though she didn't know exactly what sort of hero he was, since he didn't like to talk about it. Still, he was a hero, and that was enough for Emma. He had left the Navy to join the Lighthouse Service, and he had been assigned to the Point Bonita Light Station. This was a prestigious appointment, as it was the newest lighthouse in all of America, and it watched over the entrance to San Francisco Bay.

California. San Francisco. Point Bonita. Emma could

remember saying those names to herself. They had sounded fabulous! Why, the word *bonita*, for instance, meant beautiful in Spanish, and Emma had repeated it over and over to herself for the whole voyage. And so when the ship finally turned east and sailed through the Golden Gate and into San Francisco Bay, Emma crowded at the rail with everyone else. She hadn't noticed her father. He stood alone on the other side of the deck, holding a chart in front of him, looking in the direction opposite from everyone else, away from the shining, new city ahead, staring back over at the high, barren hills to the west, and a little bit north.

For everyone else though, the sudden appearance of a city after three months at sea was nothing short of magical. Emma blinked once or twice to make sure she wasn't imagining it. But, there it was, gleaming in the sun. Their captain gave the command to drop anchor. They had arrived.

And what a city it was. People from all over the world, dressed in ways Emma had never seen, crowded up and down the steep sidewalks past stately granite and brick buildings. Horse-drawn wagons loaded high with goods from the planet over crowded the streets and made it hard just to cross at the corner. And to think it had sprung up almost overnight! It was *exciting*, and Emma had a grand time that first day of their arrival, simply sitting on the balcony of her hotel, watching it all go by. It wasn't until the second day that she made a rather important discovery.

The second day after their arrival was the day the Green family was to leave the hotel. They were leaving to officially take up residence at the Point Bonita Light Station. And so, just after breakfast on that second day, Emma's parents went to the front desk of the hotel to settle their account. As Emma waited, she happened to wander outside to the front steps to watch the baggage man load the family's luggage onto a cart. She stood on the steps, and her eyes wandered away from the luggage and out over the streets, enjoying how splendidly, how gloriously, her new city ran up and down hills, for as far as she could see. She tried to guess which hill was closest to the water, for she knew at least that the lighthouse, her lighthouse, was on a high hill overlooking the bay.

Just at that moment, she heard someone say, "Seven hills, just like Rome." It was an old, creaking voice, and Emma looked about and saw that it was the baggage man who spoke to her.

"I beg your pardon?" she said politely.

The old man had a wrinkled face, and his watery, blue eyes peered weakly out from behind a nest of untidy, gray whiskers. He had only one tooth, which was brown, and he was smiling with it in a way that Emma hoped, anyway, was friendly. "Seven hills?" she repeated.

"Yep, just like Rome," the man said again. Then he raised his arm and with his finger slowly drew a line from south to north, stopping every so often as he recited, "Mount Davidson, Twin Peaks, Mount Sutro, Nob Hill, Russian Hill, Telegraph Hill. And this one here we're standing on is called Rincon Hill. That makes seven. 'Course, they're gonna tear this one down, make it so you don't have to walk over it just fer' to get downtown. Ain't that something? Progress, you know. So it's seven hills now, but it's soon to be six. I suppose you could throw in that hill over there, south a ways, if you really had to have seven, though it's not part of the city, not yet, it's called—"

"Bonita?" Emma suddenly suggested.

"Why, uh, no. It's just called Goat Hill."

"Oh," said Emma. And then, after reflecting for a

13

moment, she said, "So where is the one called Bonita?"

"Bonita?" said the man. "There isn't one called Bonita, so far as I know."

"There isn't? Point Bonita? That's where I'm going to live."

"*Point* Bonita. Well, that's different, young lady, why that's...," and the man started to wave to someplace far off, to the west and north, but he gave up after a second or two and scratched his head, saying, "Now, what're ya' movin' out there for? It's awfully far away."

"It is?" said Emma. This was the last thing she expected to hear, and she was much taken aback. "How far?"

"Oh, goodness, young lady," said the old man, "Awfully far. I mean, only twelve miles as the crow flies. But fer the rest of us, who ain't got wings, it sure ain't easy to get to. First, you got to find a boat to take you across the bay to Sausalito. And then you'll still have to hire horses – or walk – another... must be, ten miles. There ain't even a road, I don't think. No one lives out there."

"Really?" said Emma, almost in a squeak. "No one? No one at all? No kids or anybody?"

"Kids?" the old man snorted. "Of course not – why there's no one there at all!" He must not have been aware he was alarming the poor girl. In fact, it seemed he was only just starting to warm up to the task of speaking really badly about the place. "Depending on the weather, it can take days to get there. There's no stores, no houses, no school, no nothin'! And you'll never have visitors. Never! Why, it's the loneliest, the most desolate place I ever seen. The wind blows all day long, and in the summer it's just foggy and cold – so foggy you don't see the sun for weeks at a time. Why, you might say, it's the very ends of the earth!"

Emma looked about her at the hustle and bustle of the city. She looked behind her at the gleaming hotel and the elegant ladies and handsome gentlemen who went up and down its steps. She looked at the hotel next to it and the one next to that. And for the first time since her mother and father had told her of their plans to move to California, did she really consider what it would mean to be away from her warm home in Rhode Island, to be away from her school, to be away from her friends. For a second, she thought she actually might cry. She let out a sniffle, but put her fist to her eye to stifle it. She turned away from the old man without saying goodbye, not sure if she should even thank him for his information. In a daze, she wandered back inside the hotel where she found her mother and father still at the front desk. She didn't wait until they were done, but tugged at one's sleeve and then the other's, until they finally looked down at her to see what she wanted. And when they did, she said as bravely as she could, though with an unmistakable tremble in her voice, "B-But I thought you said we were going to live in San Francisco!"

That had all happened four days before. Already four days had gone by! Emma reminded herself though that her father had agreed to hold the post of lighthouse keeper for four years. She sighed and put her journal in the drawer under the desk. The sun was going down. She could see an orange glimmer under a dark line of rain clouds. A storm must be on the way, coming in off the big, empty Pacific Ocean. With any luck, it wouldn't hit until later that night, when she was snug in her bed. In the meantime, she said to herself, "Well, it's suppertime, and the end of one more day."

The Mystery of Rascal Pratt

- 2 -
Sammy and Sammy

    The lighthouse at Point Bonita was not at all like the lighthouses Emma had known back in Rhode Island. There had been a lighthouse not too far from where she lived. That lighthouse was rather like any other house, only it had a light-tower attached, and the keeper's family lived downstairs. Emma had never paid much attention to it – it was just part of the town.

    But at Point Bonita, no one actually lived in the light-house. For that, there was another house, the 'main house,' and it was about fifteen minutes away. To get to the light-house from the main house, you had to walk down a long, steep hill until you came to a narrow trail. The trail ran along a high cliff which overlooked a little cove. Eventually the trail led to an iron door in the face of the cliff. The door opened into a tunnel. And the tunnel burrowed through the cliff completely to the other side. There the trail picked up again, now running against the cliff a hundred feet or so above the actual ocean. Eventually it arrived at a high, wooden bridge. And of course, you had to cross the bridge. The bridge swayed back and forth over the most violent and fearsome waves Emma had ever seen. Only then did you arrive at the lighthouse itself, which was perched way up on a high, nee-dle-shaped spire of green and gray rock. The whole thing was beyond anything in Emma's imagination, and she wondered how on earth anyone had ever built the place to begin with.

But they had, and there it was, and there Emma was too, sitting at a desk in the light tower, in front of her now twice-closed journal which she had just shut with its final, little thump. Aside from Emma, the lighthouse was empty. Emma's father had left earlier in the day on an errand, and Emma's mother, who had filled in for her husband and had done much of the evening's work – winding the weights, pol-ishing the globes, trimming the wicks – had already returned to the main house. Emma, however, had decided she wanted to stay behind in the lighthouse for a bit, even though of recent it made her uneasy to be alone. But now, she had fin-ished her journal entry, which, as already noted, was exactly like the entry her father had made that day in his log. She was just getting ready to leave when she happened to look up and see the machinery of the lens and the shade whir-ring above her head, in the highest part of the light tower.

The lens turned round and round, brighter, darker, brighter again, in its steady pattern. Outside, the wind moaned and buffeted the tower, but inside, the whirring of the machinery seemed warm and peaceful. Quite in spite of herself, Emma found she almost liked it. She smiled and then turned and went out the door.

She shut the door behind her, and as she stood on the stone platform which surrounded the whole lighthouse like a porch, a cold gust of wind nearly blew her down. It blew Emma's hair into her face and mouth. A few drops of rain spattered down around her, blowing practically sideways, stinging her cheeks and the corners of her eyes. Emma pulled her oilskin coat more tightly around her and made her way to the wooden bridge which connected the lighthouse to the rest of the world. It swayed as she took her first step. Waves crashed below her with a mighty wallop, much louder than the thump made by the closing of her father's log. The air was filled with cries of wild animals – sea lions* and sea birds. She clenched harder at the cable that served as the handrail and closed her eyes. She opened them again and hurried quickly across.

All right, she thought, now the tunnel. For her first few days, she had found the tunnel to be spooky, particularly at night. But this evening, with the lantern in hand and several days under her belt, and the bridge safely behind her, she actually felt braver. As always, big shadows jumped out at her from

---

*There are three kinds of seals that are natives to San Francisco Bay: the harbor seal, the northern sea lion (also called Steller's sea lion), and the California sea lion. At one time, there was also the northern fur seal and the fantastical elephant seal, almost the size of a small whale, but both of these have been hunted nearly out of existence and live on remote islands off the coast. (E.G.)

the wall, but by now she was starting to know them all and to expect them. The scary shadow from the rock on the right, just after the first bend, she called "Big Bear." And the next shadow, which looked just like the first, only much smaller, she called "Baby Bear." And just like that, she was done with the tunnel. She closed the iron door behind her.

After the tunnel, she still had the steep walk up the hill to the house. But suddenly feeling a little more confident, a  little more independent than usual, she turned her collar up and started off. However, it wasn't long before she heard the trees in a nearby grove of cypress and pine creaking in the wind. She immediately recalled the croaking voice of the old baggage man back in San Francisco. She could almost hear him saying, "It's cold. It's desolate. It's the ends of the earth," and from somewhere not far away, a night bird cried out in its eerie voice. Emma put her head down and walked faster, trying her best not to run. When she got to the house, she stepped inside and quickly closed the door.

She hung up her oilskin coat. She noticed that her father's coat was also hung on a peg, which meant that he too must be home. She went to the kitchen. A gas lamp was lit on the table, but no one was there.

"Mama?" she called, "Papa?"

"We're in here, Emma," her mother answered. Her voice came from the room they called "the parlor." The parlor was a sitting room furnished with a few wooden chairs, and also, somehow, with a sofa. Emma always marveled that such a thing was brought way out here from San Francisco. The parlor had a fireplace too, and that night, her mother had lit a fire in it. Both her parents were sitting in front of it.

20

In looks, Emma's mother, Mabel, was essentially the grown-up version of Emma – aside from Emma's braids, anyway. She was a schoolteacher by profession, or she had been rather, back in Rhode Island. She was also a painter – a dabbler in oils especially – and unlike Emma, she seemed thrilled at the wild remoteness of her new surroundings. Even though the family had been at Point Bonita only a few days, Mabel Green could often be found setting up her easel here and there, making preliminary sketches of the bluffs, of the cove, and so on. And while she might have lost some of the appearance of youth to her long dress and starched collar, instead of the cotton pinafore that Emma wore, there was still a mischievous twinkle to her chestnut eyes that no amount of starched collar could hide, and they shined out at Emma, even then, in the firelight.

Beside Mrs. Green sat Emma's father, Captain Green. His eyes didn't gleam nearly so keenly. They were warm and blue to be sure, but they had a tired look, as though they had squinted too many times into wind and sun and cannon fire. Also, there was a sort of a heaviness to them, as is often the case of those who have seen too much suffering.

He kept his thick hair neatly cropped. This was a habit left over from years in the military, and he wore a short, stiff beard. He remained very much the sea captain, though he was on land now, and he seemed hardly able to spend more than a few minutes without glancing at the sky for some sign of a coming change in weather.

Emma started to ask her mother and father what they were doing sitting in the dark, no lamps lit, their faces illuminated only by the flicker of the fire. But then she noticed a box on the floor in front of them and she also noticed how each of her parents stole a glance into it. Emma walked over to peak inside too. Something squeaked. Emma jumped back. Her mother and father laughed.

"Emma," said Captain Green, "I'd like you to meet your new friend." He reached into the box and gently lifted out a puppy. The little animal whimpered and Captain Green held it out to his daughter. "Emma, meet Sammy."

The puppy was very small. He was dark mostly, with soft fur. His belly was white and he also had a thin white stripe that ran between his eyes down to a pointed, little nose. His ears almost stood up. He smelled like milk.

"Your father got him on the road coming back from Sausalito," said Mrs. Green.

Captain Green nodded. "I met an old man, an Indian I think. He must live near here, and he was selling them. He called this one 'Sammy'."

Emma took the little dog from him. She didn't know why, but before she could do anything about it, a tear came to her eye. "Sammy," she whispered. And with a smile, she wiped away the tear on the back of her wrist and rubbed the little dog's face to hers.

Over the next few days, Emma and Sammy became fast friends. They went everywhere together – out to the lighthouse to visit Captain Green, down to the cove below the house, or out to the bluffs where Mrs. Green set up her easel to paint whenever there was a sunset. One evening, just after dinner, while there was still a good bit of light in the sky, Emma and Sammy walked up the path in the other direction, away from the ocean. They walked along aimlessly. Emma had no special place to go, and she was content just to follow Sammy, laughing every so often at his clumsy antics – for instance when he stopped to poke his head into someone else's burrow and then had to remove it rather quickly. As they walked, Emma lost track of time. It wasn't long before they were actually a goodly ways from home. Emma suddenly sensed this and stopped to look around. It occurred to her that she had never been so far away from the house by herself. The breeze off the ocean now seemed to moan a little more mournfully than it had just moments before, and a stand of nearby trees creaked with a sound Emma didn't care for at all. She called to Sammy, "Here boy, let's go home." But at that very moment, Sammy yelped and ran away from her, and away from home, as fast as his legs could carry him.

Emma ran after him, shouting, "Sammy! Sammy, this way! Come back!" but Sammy ran on, getting farther and farther away until he disappeared over the top of the hill. Emma looked behind her. By then she was almost a mile from home. But she couldn't go back without Sammy. She gathered her skirt and ran as fast as she could, huffing and puffing, up the hill, and then down again the other side.

She came to a small grove of dry oak trees that was in a protected, little nook in the hillside. "Sammy?" she called. She listened, but hearing nothing in return, she pushed on through the trees, ducking under the lowest branches. She came out the other side and there in front of her was an old, ramshackle fence. It was a little corral, almost completely falling apart. There were no cows or horses or any other kind of livestock in the corral. But there was Sammy and, to Emma's surprise, he wasn't alone. He was wrestling with another little dog that looked almost exactly like him.

But that wasn't all. A boy and girl were also there, sitting on their knees, looking up in astonishment at Emma. They both looked like they were Emma's same age. The boy was wearing long canvas trousers and leather, lace-up work shoes.

He had on a cotton shirt and over it he wore a pair of suspenders which held his trousers up. His hair was red, and just under his eyes, spangled from cheek to cheek over the bridge of his nose, was a thick mask of freckles.

The girl sitting next to him wore a calico dress and a cotton pinafore not too different in style from Emma's, though this new girl's had been patched many times. She too had on a pair of low, lace-up boots; in fact, they were identical to the boy's, if a good bit more beaten up. Of the three children, she was probably the tallest. Her skin was somewhat darker than either Emma's or the boy's, and she wore her hair, which was jet black, over her shoulder in a shiny ponytail. For a long while the three children simply looked at each other. Finally, the boy said, "Good evening."

"Oh, hi there," said Emma, "I'm sorry for intruding. I was just looking for my dog. Come here, Sammy."

But Sammy paid Emma no attention.

The boy did however, and he said, "Sammy? That's funny. Is your dog Sammy, too? Sammy is the name of my dog." He chuckled and pointed to the two dogs playing in front of him. "I thought they looked like they knew each other. You must have gotten your dog from Achilles."

"Achilles?" said Emma. "I don't know – my father got him on the way home from Sausalito. He said he bought him from an old Indian."

"Sure," said the boy, "that was Achilles. And this is his granddaughter. This is Sue. Sue Hermanastra."

The girl, Sue, nodded, but otherwise said nothing.

Until that moment, Emma had only known of Indians from books. She wondered if she shouldn't have said something like 'My father bought him from a man by the side of the road,' instead of "an old Indian." She stammered, "O-oh, hi, my name's Emma. So that was your... well, please tell him I love Sammy. He's become a wonderful friend."

Sue studied Emma for a second or two. "They make good work dogs too," she said plainly.

It fell quiet again, until after a few awkward seconds the boy said, "Say, Sue, my dog's name is Sammy, and now it turns out that this girl's dog is Sammy too. Does Achilles name all the dogs Sammy?"

Sue laughed. "How long have you known Achilles? 'Sammee' is how he says 'puppy' in his language – Sammee, it just means *little dog*."

The boy also laughed and said sheepishly, "Really? Well, I guess I never knew that." Then, addressing Emma he said, "By the way, my name is Harris. Harris Cole. My pa is Edgar Cole – I expect you've heard of him." He stuck his thumbs proudly in the straps that held up his trousers.

Actually, Emma had not heard of Edgar Cole. The look on her face must have said so, since the boy, Harris, explained, "He owns this here rancho*. He's famous. He's a hero, wounded and all, from fightin' Indians."

"Oh, I see," said Emma. "Well, nice to meet you," though this second mention of Indians made her feel a little uneasy, again not sure what was polite. "Nice to meet you *both*." She

---

*Here's something interesting I learned: in the early days of the colonization of California, much of the countryside was divided up into ranchos. Ranchos were enormous pieces of land given by the Spanish and Mexican governments to individual pioneers if they promised to farm or ranch them. The pioneers could be from anywhere in the world, and they were all given Mexican citizenship (and the title "Don") prior to receiving the land. Many of the new dons around San Francisco were actually from the United States. When the United States took over California after the Mexican-American war, the American government honored the original land grants. *(E.G.)*

stepped out from under the trees a little more. "My name is Emma Green. My father is Captain Green, the new lighthouse keeper."

"Oh yeah," said Harris. "They just finished building the new lighthouse, didn't they? The old one didn't work too well, I hear – too high up on the hill and always hidden by fog. In the summer, it's so foggy here. Why you can go for— "

"Weeks," interrupted Emma, "*weeks* without seeing the sun."

"I was going to say months," said Harris, "but, same difference. Anyway, is your father really a captain? Are all lighthouse keepers captains?"

"Come to think of it, I don't know," said Emma, "My father was a sea captain before this." She was overcome with a proud feeling of her own and wished she had suspenders to stick her thumbs behind. She stuck her thumbs behind the top of her pinafore, just to try it out and added, "In fact, he was a captain in the U.S. Navy and a hero too, a hero in the Civil War."

"Gosh," said Harris, who was obviously impressed, "I believe if I was a sea captain and a hero in the war, I'd stay on as a sea captain. I wouldn't quit it for nothing. Life as a lighthouse keeper must be awfully lonely."

At this, Emma drew in a sharp breath. The truth was, she had been thinking something along these same lines herself, though she hadn't yet put it so plainly. She did wonder why her father had left the Navy, where he was admired and respected. She never quite understood the explanations he had given her, and then, out of the blue, he had taken this new job, way out here in California, just about as far away from their old lives – and from everything else – as possible. It had all happened so quickly. But she couldn't tell all this

Sammy and Sammy

to a boy and girl she had only just met. "Well, he didn't quit," she said, "He retired."

"Right, that's what I mean, *retired*," said Harris. "Still, I don't know if I would have done that either."

Once again a silence fell on the group. Emma turned to the other girl, to Sue Hermanastra, thinking it would be polite to include her. "So, Sue – what about your father? He sells dogs?" The moment Emma said this, she wished she hadn't. It was ridiculous – she had never in her whole life heard of a dog-trader.

"Well, first of all, Achilles is my *grand*father," said Sue, correcting Emma on a completely different point. "My father and my mother died... not too long ago."

"Oh goodness, I'm sorry to hear that!" exclaimed Emma, and to herself she thought, "What's the matter with me – I can't say anything right!"

"Achilles does a lot more than sell dogs," put in Harris. "He works for my father. He's been on the rancho since before I was born. He's my father's right hand-man. He's important out here."

"I guess you could say that." said Sue. She was poking the ground with a twig at that moment. "But, suppose we talk about something else, can we?" And looking up, she said, "So, Emma, do you like to read?"

"Me?" said Emma. "Sure, who doesn't?"

"Well, Harris here wouldn't read if you paid him."

"So what?" said Harris. "Who wants to read any of those nonsense books of yours, those bratty English kids or whoever they are, traveling around Europe on trains, listening to rich people's conversations."

"They're solving *mysteries*," said Sue as she rolled her eyes.

"Right, mysteries," said Harris. Then turning to Emma, he said, "Sue is always talking about England and France. It's the only thing she thinks about. She says when she grows up she's going to Europe to be a famous dancer."

Looking at Sue, Emma could easily imagine her as a dancer in the ballet, with her long, thin limbs. There was an air of maturity and poise about her too. "Well, I do like to read," Emma said, "though I haven't really read any mysteries."

"Oh, they're fun," said Sue. "You should try them. In fact, I always wanted to have a little mystery-solving club, like the kids in those books that Harris was just talking about. It would sure make life more exciting."

"There aren't any mysteries out here," said Harris, glancing about them. "And thank goodness, I say. The Cole family never would've got a fine rancho like this solving mysteries. No sir, it's all about hard work!"

"Everything's a mystery," said Sue quietly. "Today we solved the mystery of the two Sammies." She laughed suddenly, and Harris and Emma did too.

"Well, I'm game," said Emma. "Let's form a club."

"What about you, Harris?" said Sue.

"Oh, I suppose I'll join too."

"Well, don't let us force you!" said Sue. But to Emma, she winked and added, "Very good – sounds like we're all in. Let's meet here tomorrow, same time!"

As Emma walked home that evening, she carried Sammy, her Sammy, under her arm so he wouldn't run away. It was genuinely dark by then. The sun finished its setting before she was halfway home. Trees in the little stands of pine and cypress creaked as she passed.* A few drops of rain spattered

---

*The cypress here are formally known as Monterey Cypress. They are low conifers, like a cedar, and they were planted up and down the

on her face. The wind moaned over the hills. But now Emma walked directly into it. It was fresh; it smelled of the sea. She had warm, little Sammy under her arm, and somewhere behind her were two new friends. Nearby, an owl hooted. Only, when it did, Emma no longer heard the voice of the old baggage man.

---

coast by ranchers in the middle of this century to form windbreaks. Some people don't like them as they aren't native plants, but I do. I like their little cones and how the hawks and such seem to like to rest on them. For me they are part of the landscape, certainly as much as I am myself. *(E.G.)*

The Mystery of Rascal Pratt

- 3 -

The Arrival

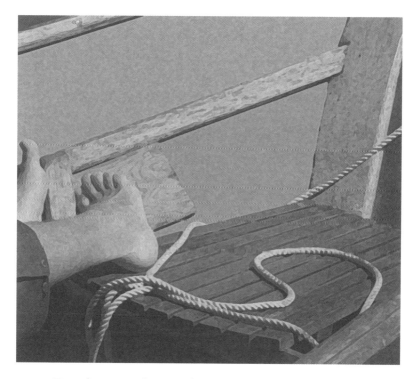

For the next few weeks, Emma and Harris and Sue worked on many mysteries. Harris almost always thought they had solved them by the time it got dark and they all had to go back to their homes. Sue almost always thought they hadn't, and Emma was never quite sure. They knew of course that the mysteries they worked on were all just for play, until one day that is, when something of real interest – and not to just themselves, but even to the grown-ups around – truly did happen.

The three children happened to be down on a small, pebble beach not too far below the path that ran from the main house along the cliffs to the lighthouse. The beach was on the protected waters of a little cove, and since it faced east, it was sheltered from large winter waves and also from the northwest wind by the towering rocks and cliffs of Point Bonita. The cove and the little pebble beach, being the only place around that was even passably warm, as it was out of the wind and often in sunshine, had become headquarters for many of the games the three friends played.

That day the weather was clear, beautifully clear, and it was windless too, the only really windless day Emma could remember since she and her family had moved to Point Bonita. The air smelled of the first perfume of spring flowers, and the sun bounced merrily off the waters of the cove. Just as the friends finished eating their lunches, Emma happened to spy something drifting around the point into the cove. With her hand, she shielded her eyes against the glare. The thing drifted closer.

"That's odd," she said. "Is that a boat? No one's in it." She stood and pointed across the cove. Sue and Harris stood up too. It was now obvious that the thing was a boat. It was a little rowboat, in fact, a dory*, as that sort of boat is called, with plain plank sides and a pointed front. It was leaning badly to one side and appeared to be damaged in the front, or the bow.

"I believe it *is*," said Harris, standing up and shading his

---

*A dory is a small, light rowboat with angular sides, popular among fisherman because they can be stacked on the deck of a larger boat and can carry tremendous loads of fish. They are also popular boats for children because they have a stable, flat bottom. (*E.G.*)

eyes too. "I'd like a little boat. Let's see if we can get it." And with that he took off his shoes and socks and waded out into  the water. Only the first few yards out from shore were shallow. Harris walked out as far as he dared, but when it became clear that he wouldn't be able to reach the boat by himself, Sue took off her shoes too and from shallower water held onto his arm to help him balance. Emma watched for a few seconds, then put her shoes right next to Sue's and followed them both, though she didn't go so deep. She couldn't swim very well, and also she was afraid of waves, even the tiny ones that lapped the shore there in the cove. Sammy, however, stayed on the beach and yipped in his gruff, little voice.

The dory drifted closer, but it stayed in deep water. A fresh gust of wind would have sent it sailing past them and beyond their reach, but Harris leapt and somehow caught hold of it. It was a mighty jump. His head bobbed under the cold water of San Francisco Bay, but he came up sputtering, and through it all, he managed to hold onto the boat.

"Take my hand," Sue shouted. She reached out and caught Harris's free hand. And Emma held onto Sue's arm. Like that, the three of them caught the dory.

They pulled it back towards the beach. Once they were in shallow water again and could see over its wooden rail, they looked inside. They gasped. They had expected to see a tangle of rope and they certainly would not have been surprised to also find a jumble of sail-canvas and a broken oar. Indeed, they saw all this. But also, and very much to their astonishment, on all the other debris, lay a boy. He seemed about their size. The side of his face bore an ugly wound, and by all appearances, he was dead, or deep in an unnatural sleep.

Five minutes later, Emma burst into the lantern room of the lighthouse. She was out of breath and still dripping wet.

"Papa, Papa!" she called between breaths. "A boat! A boat drifted into the cove. We pulled it up to the beach. Papa, come quick, there's a boy in it!"

Her father was high up in the works of the lighttower. "What's that you say?" he called down. "I didn't see a boat."

"I think it drifted in along the cliffs. It's a wonder the waves didn't break it on the rocks."

Captain Green climbed down the ladder. "Where is it now? The cove?"

When they got back down to the cove, they found that Harris and Sue had pulled the dory higher up onto the beach.

"Well, I'll be!" exclaimed Captain Green in a low voice, when he looked inside, "It *is* a boy," and he bent down to look more closely.

"He's breathing, sir," said Sue.

The captain nodded. "All right, let's get him to the house. Now, Harris, Sue, do either of you know the doctor in Sausalito?"

"Yes, sir," said Harris, "we do, but that's a long way from here."

"Yes, it is," agreed the captain with a nod. "All right, here's what we'll do then: you and Sue run back to the rancho. If anyone is riding into town today, have them take a message to the doctor. Tell him we've found a young boy, a shipwreck survivor from the looks of it. Mr. Cole or Mr. Achilles should be able to find someone to go, but Harris, Sue – you'll have to press upon them the importance – understand?"

"Yes, sir!" both Harris and Sue said at the same time, and they ran off as fast as they could. It was a long way to the rancho, and much, much farther still to Sausalito, the better part of a day's journey. Emma knew it would be a long while before any doctor got the message. Captain Green lifted the boy gently out of the dory. And with Emma and Sammy following behind, he carried him up the path to the main house, to the second floor, where there was an empty bedroom.

Emma's mother rushed upstairs to join them when she heard the commotion. When she saw the boy on the bed, she bent over to have a look at him. She recoiled and said, "Oh my, what happened to his face?"

"Who can say?" said the captain. "But we should clean it." As a lighthouse officer, Captain Green kept a small kit of medical supplies. He fetched it from downstairs and then he and Mrs. Green cleaned the wound. "It's very curious, this injury," he said. "It looks like two wounds. There's this cut, you see, then, there's a burn underneath. Wait – it's hard to see with all the scabbing, but, look here, is that a brand?"

The two looked at the wound more closely. They exchanged a glance that made Emma wonder if they knew something they didn't want to say out loud.

"Say, Emma?" said Captain Green at that very moment, as though he guessed her suspicion, "Could you run get one of your nightshirts? We will dress him in that. We should get him out of this wet clothing."

Emma hesitated, then did as her father bid. When she came back with the nightshirt, Captain Green was saying to Mrs. Green, "It looks like his leg is broken too. This poor fellow has seen quite a bit of trouble. If it's to heal right, the doctor will have to come soon." He shook his head and carried on changing the boy into the nightshirt as gently as he could. Then, he and Mrs. Green got him back into the bed and tried to make him comfortable.

For a while, they all stood around looking at him, until after some time Captain Green said he wanted to go look at the boy's rowboat, down in the cove. Perhaps it bore some mark that would give them a clue as to where the boy came from. "I'll be back directly. Emma, why don't you sit in that chair and if the boy starts to wake, call us."

He and Mrs. Green left the room. Once they were outside and headed down the stairs though, Emma could hear them speaking in hushed voices, and she wondered what they were not telling her. She sat down in the chair. Sammy curled up on the floor at her feet. After a few minutes, she got up to look at the boy more closely. He wasn't big at all. In fact, he was no bigger than she, and maybe even smaller. He had dark hair – it was tangled and hopelessly matted. His skin looked as though it had been burnt brown by many years in the sun. On his face was the wound her parents had spoken of. They were right – it did look terrible. Emma hoped that Harris and Sue would find a rider soon to take the message to the doctor. She sat back in her chair and waited.

The room was warm and quiet. It was heavy with sleep from the breathing of the mysterious boy. After a little while, Emma began to notice that her head nodded and her eyelids had become heavy too, though it would have been very unusual for her to doze off in the middle of the afternoon. All the same, she closed her eyes – it was just to rest them, and for the briefest little moment – when she realized Sammy was growling, and not only that, but he had been growling for some time! She lifted her head with a jerk. At first she thought she was dreaming, as she saw the strange boy standing directly in front of her, peering at her as though in a daze. He balanced precariously on his one good leg. Emma was startled to see him, just gazing at her from so close. He had an empty expression on his face, like he was sleepwalking.

"Hello?" said Emma, and she stood up quickly.

The boy took a step back, as if he were startled too, but he put his weight on his bad leg and instantly fell down on the floor in pain. Emma reached out to help him. But the boy pushed himself away from her, crawling across the floor, as though he were frightened of her. And as he did, he began to shout in a funny, lilting accent, "Stay away from me! Where have you taken me? Where is my ship?"

Sammy barked ferociously from his hiding place behind Emma's skirt. She tried to stop him and at the same time, calm the boy.

But the boy would not be calmed. "Stay away!" he yelled. "I'm Rascal Pratt, the pirate, the *famous* pirate! Stay away, I'm warning you!"

At that moment, Emma's parents rushed into the room. "What's happening up here?" her father demanded.

For a second or so the boy stopped his screaming. He looked at the family – Emma, her mother, and her father – and then he started to shout even more wildly than before. "Stay away from me, I say! Stay away!" he shouted, over and over again.

"It's all right," said Captain Green gently, "you're safe here."

But it seemed as though it was Captain Green who frightened the boy especially, since he continued to shout, saying, "Stay away from me, sir, your uniform gives you away!" He became more excited with every minute, until Emma thought that certainly something dreadful would happen. And indeed, after many rounds of this sort of ranting, the boy simply collapsed.

Captain Green and Mrs. Green looked at the poor heap on the floor. Without a word, they moved him back to the bed. They stood beside him and watched him with concern, until Captain Green said, "A broken leg, an infected wound, and who knows how many days in the open ocean in that little boat – the madness is no wonder. I certainly hope the doctor gets here quickly."

- 4 -

Facts and Fevers

The following day the fog came in. Emma woke to the drip-drip-drip of water trickling off the roof one drop at a time. At first, she even thought it was raining. But when she got up and looked out her window, she saw that a low, thick cloud of fog covered the world outside with fine droplets. A chill breeze off the ocean sent shivers through everything, even the bushes. It was as dreary a morning as the day before had been fine and sparkling.

Emma rubbed her eyes, then turned away from the window and got dressed, with the idea of checking on the injured boy, Rascal Pratt, as he had called himself, before she went downstairs. Before she left her room though, she happened to glance out the window again, and when she did, she noticed for the first time that there was a sailing vessel anchored in the cove. It wasn't very big, forty feet long at the most, and it had a single mast and two booms – one for each of the main and the fore sails. It was anchored not far from shore, and from her room, she could see a small crew of men busily unloading barrels from its deck into a rowboat at its side. Emma wondered what it could be.

She went downstairs. Her parents were in the kitchen. Her father had just come inside, and as Emma entered the room, he was taking off his coat and saying to Mrs. Green, "Did you see that cutter in the cove? It's a supply boat from the Lighthouse Service. I was hoping for fuel for the lanterns and staples for the kitchen here, but it's brought us a load of ammunition for the fog gun!"

"Ammunition?" said Emma's mother, pouring a cup of coffee for her husband. "Fog gun?"

"Oh, there's an old artillery cannon that's been gathering dust in the machinery room out at the lighthouse. I'm supposed to fire it when the fog is in, to warn ships off the rocks. Just powder, no shot, it's just for the noise. I haven't dragged it out yet, because we haven't had much fog– in fact, today's the first I've seen of it. Plus it's bound to drive us all mad, a cannon going off every ninety minutes, all summer long." He shook his head. "Well, anyway, there's an eager young fellow in command of the cutter. He's a lieutenant in the Lighthouse Service and very much wants to make a name for himself. He's from a wealthy family back east. Walker's his name and his family is footing the bill to arm all the old fog guns in San Francisco with live ammunition – twenty-five pound balls! The first line of coastal defense, they're calling it, in case we come under attack."

"Attack?" said Mrs. Green, now pouring coffee for herself. "From whom?"

Captain Green shrugged and sighed wearily. Apparently he had been having the same discussion with the men outside. About then, Emma's parents noticed her standing in the doorway. She had been listening quietly as she wanted to find out more about the fog cannon since, like her mother, this was the first she had heard of it. Anything new out at Point Bonita was always of interest.

But before she could ask, Mrs. Green said, "Good morning, dear, any news from our new young guest?" Mrs. Green meant Rascal Pratt of course.

"Oh, no," said Emma with a frown and coming the rest of the way into the kitchen. "Not a peep. I wonder how long he can sleep."

"I wonder who he is," said Mrs. Green.

"You know, I did take a closer look at his little dory," said Captain Green. "There are no marks on it that I could find. It's strange."

"Well, he says he's a pirate," said Emma with a laugh. "Can you imagine?"

Emma's mother shook her head and her father said, "I wouldn't make anything of it. That's just the fever talking."

Still, Emma found it very puzzling, even if it was only the fever. She couldn't help but wonder what had happened to the boy. She sat down to eat breakfast and, as she did, she turned this question over in her head, as well as some others she had, mainly questions about the news of the fog gun.

A short while later, there came a knock at the front door.

Emma started to get out of her seat to answer it, but Captain Green got to it first. It turned out to be the doctor. He introduced himself and apologized for the lateness of his arrival, explaining that he had ridden from Sausalito as early as he could. The captain thanked him for making such haste anyway and immediately showed him upstairs. Emma got up from the table and ran after them. She reached the top of the stairs just as Captain Green was opening the door to Rascal Pratt's room. But seeing his daughter, he said, "Wait downstairs, Emma. Why don't you... why don't you take the doctor's horse to the watering trough?" And without waiting for an answer, he closed the door behind him.

Emma sighed, but she ran downstairs and out the front door as fast as she could. As usual, Sammy was at her heels. The doctor's horse was hitched to the fence near the house. Emma unhitched him and led him around back, towards the little stable where her father kept his mule and her mother kept some chickens. She quickly pumped water from the cistern* into the watering trough and then turned to run back to the house. But as she did, a high-pitched scream came from an open window on the second floor. It was a horrible yell, one of great pain. At the sound, the doctor's horse jumped, Sammy spun around, and Emma's hair stood on end. But then it was quiet again and she heard nothing more.

"Rascal Pratt!" she cried under her breath, and she dropped her pail and ran back across the yard to the kitchen, through the parlor and up the stairs. But she was met by her father, and the doctor as well, who were coming down. "Emma? Didn't I ask you to stay downstairs?" said Captain

---

*There isn't much water out at Point Bonita – or lots of other places in California – so we catch rainwater and save it in big tanks called "cisterns." *(E.G.)*

42

Green sternly. "You ought not have heard that. Setting a broken leg is a painful thing. I thought you were tending to the doctor's horse."

"But I was – I mean, I am," stammered Emma.

"Well then, would you please fetch him back to the front?"

So Emma ran back down the stairs once more and cutting through the parlor again to the kitchen, she started to leave the house by the back door. The captain, in the meanwhile, led the doctor downstairs into the parlor where they both sat down, as though to discuss something important. When Emma saw this, she stopped and lingered for an extra moment outside the house.

The doctor had just started to speak, but the captain stopped him and leaning forward in his chair, he looked through the kitchen, through the back door to the back steps where he saw Emma standing and listening. "The doctor's horse, Emma," said Captain Green, "if you would be so kind."

So Emma sighed, then bounded down the back steps, back out into the yard, over to the stable, untied the reins of the doctor's horse from the post at the watering trough, and led him back around to the front where she tied him again to the fence in front of the house. She waited for what seemed forever. Finally her father came out the front door. He wore a troubled look on his face. The doctor followed closely behind.

"Thank you, young lady," said the doctor to Emma, as he took the reins to his horse. Emma watched as he and Captain Green strolled a short distance away from the house, with the horse walking slowly behind them.

Just then, another man appeared on the path that ran

out to the lighthouse. Emma did not recognize him. Like her father, he wore the uniform of the Lighthouse Service. But he was much younger, perhaps by as many as fifteen years. He had a fair complexion, a smallish nose and largish chin. He was passably handsome and cultivated a stylish pair of sideburns. His build was athletic, and he walked rapidly and assuredly into the yard from the direction of cove, up to Captain Green and the doctor, who stopped talking as soon as they heard his footsteps.

"You're all set, Captain Green," said the man. "We brought your gun out of retirement. She's on the platform now, just outside the light tower, so you can get to her easily. There's a keg of powder in the magazine, plus a few rounds of ammunition."

Captain Green looked at the younger man without saying anything. At length though, he turned to the doctor and said, "Doctor, allow me to introduce Lieutenant Walker, U.S. Lighthouse Service. He's re-supplying all the old fog cannons up and down the coast."

The doctor nodded pleasantly.

"Well, these aren't just fog cannons," said Lieutenant Walker taking a step closer and wagging a finger. "The fog cannons are real guns. I'm stocking every lighthouse on the coast with a few rounds of live ammunition. My father's company, back east, is picking up the tab. It's California's first line of defense! Now, Captain Green, I've left you three rounds of ammunition. It isn't much, but I've several other batteries to get to. I'll bring more next month."

"Thank your father for me, Lieutenant," said Captain Green, tipping his hat. Then he turned to the doctor and said, "Lieutenant Walker suffered the great misfortune of missing the last war entirely. But, he's eager to be of service now."

At this, Lieutenant Walker went red in the face. He stammered and said, "Well, we mustn't let down our guard. The whole coast is unprotected, as you know."

"Of course, you're right, you're right," said Captain Green, "unprotected, from the unseen enemy. And I'm sure you, and your father's company – he makes these munitions, does he not? – will see to it that no sand dune goes unprotected a day longer."

The young lieutenant started to agree before he realized that the older captain was only making fun of him again. And he protested, "Begging your pardon, Captain, but there is always a threat of some sort. Even if you don't see it, we would be wrong not to take it seriously."

The captain nodded but said nothing. The doctor however wanted to take the joke further, or so it seemed, and he said, "Just so, Lieutenant! In fact, you'll never guess who drifted into our cove only yesterday. Why, it was a *pirate*. A famous pirate at that, Rascal Pratt, if I recall the name – did I get it right, Captain?"

At this the captain cleared his throat and shot the doctor a look that meant, quite plainly, to shut up.

But it was too late, as the lieutenant was suddenly all ears. "A pirate, you say? Here? Where is he?"

The doctor glanced nervously now between the lieutenant and Captain Green, as though he didn't know what he was allowed to say or which of them he should answer.

So Captain Green said, "The doctor is just teasing you, Lieutenant. Forgive us both. A young boy, shipwrecked it seems, drifted into the cove yesterday. We don't know anything about him, except that in the height of his fever he woke and shouted that he was a pirate, then collapsed again. Pure madness of course. Fever – or thirst. I've seen it before."

But the lieutenant ignored the captain and addressed the doctor directly, "I'm sorry, *what* did you say the name was? Did you say Rascal... Rascal somebody-or-other?"

"Lieutenant," Captain Green cut in, "whatever the name, he's just a boy. A *very* young boy at that. He told the doctor just now he's sixteen, but that's obviously a fabrication. He's smaller than my daughter here. I'd say he's more likely eleven or twelve, wouldn't you, doctor? And quite probably mad, the poor chap."

"But if he claims to be a pir— " the lieutenant started to say.

Captain Green interrupted him gruffly. "Lieutenant Walker, thank you. But that's enough. He's only a boy."

The lieutenant lifted his finger as though to make one last point, stopped himself and, with a click of his heels, said instead, "Very well, Captain. At any rate, you have your cannon now. I trust you remember how to use it." With that, he bowed and walked briskly back toward the trail that led down to the cove. Just before he disappeared over the brink of the bluff he snapped his fingers, turned to face them, and called, "Rascal *Pratt*, I believe you said Doctor? Thank you, I'll keep an ear out for the name." Then he turned back to the trail and departed for good.

Emma, her father, and the doctor all watched the place where the lieutenant had disappeared, until after a few seconds the doctor said to Captain Green, "Well, if I may ask, what *do* you intend to do? You know the mark on the boy's face as well as I do. You are obliged to report the matter."

Captain Green breathed out heavily. "Yes, doctor, I understand. It's just that, this boy, this Rascal Pratt, if that's his name, seems so young. Much too young. There must be some other explanation."

"But the law is the law," said the doctor.

Captain Green started to say something, then glanced uneasily at Emma as if he had just realized she was there. He took the doctor by the arm and led him a few steps away. Emma strained her ears to hear, but try as she might, she could hear nothing more of what they said. She waited for a while as they continued talking, until finally she returned to the house and sat down in the kitchen to the last bit of her breakfast, trying to make sense of what her father had said.

A few minutes later, Captain Green, too, came back into the house. As he entered the kitchen, Emma leapt up at him without thinking and said, "Papa! Are you really going to turn Rascal Pratt in? How come?"

Captain Green looked at his daughter as though he had not expected to see her there and he said sternly, almost angrily, "Were you eavesdropping on me?"

Now, Captain Green was seldom angry – at least, Emma had not often seen him that way. Even so, she decided to press on, since the question was already half out. "But what's he done?" she said, "Is it because he's a pirate?"

At this, the frown on her father's face disappeared and was replaced by a smile. "The boy, a pirate?" he chuckled. "Goodness, no! –Emma, it's just as I was telling the doctor outside – you must distinguish between what a young boy says when he is in a fever and the l—"

Emma imagined he was going to say "the law," as he had just been speaking of it, outside with the doctor. For some reason, though, he didn't finish and suddenly seemed deep in thought.

"Between *what* and fevers?" pressed Emma.

"What's that?" said the Captain looking up after another moment, "Oh yes, well, *facts*, I suppose. You must learn to distinguish between facts and fevers. But, let's not talk about it anymore, shall we? And I promise, I won't do anything until I have all the facts myself."

- 5 -
Concerning the Names of Things

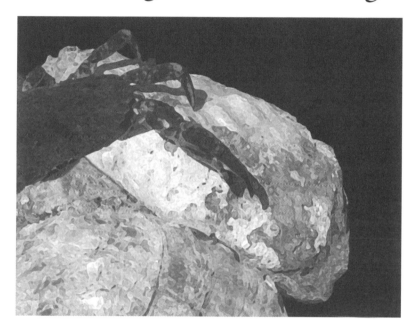

27th of April, 1866: 1 timber schooner, Arena, and the clipper, Flying Cloud, of Medford, Massachusetts. Sundry fishing vessels, all of San Francisco, and 1 of Monterey.

Emma sat at the desk in the lantern room. Her father was below in the watch-room, winding weights, and Emma was waiting for him, having promised to help him polish the globes and trim the wicks. While she waited, she copied the entry from his log into her journal, as she often did. It was brief, and when she was done, she chewed for a minute or two on the end of her pencil and then bent back over her journal and added:

It's been two weeks since Rascal Pratt arrived. He still needs crutches but seems to be on the mend. The doctor certainly did a good job setting the broken leg. But Rascal Pratt doesn't talk to anyone. When he leaves his room, he usually goes straight outdoors and stays out for hours at a time. Who knows what he is doing. I followed him once, by accident really, and found him sitting on the rocks, at the far end of the cove looking out towards the sea. He sat there for at least an hour. Maybe his leg hurts him more than he lets on.

She closed her journal, with its little *thump*, and put it back in the drawer under the desk, and as she did, she heard someone walking outside, over the bridge. It was her mother, and she had an empty, wooden bucket in her hand.

"Emma, dear, are you busy?" said Mrs. Green as she entered the lighthouse and peered up the ladder at Emma in the lantern room. "I need someone to go down to the cove to collect mussels for dinner."

Emma looked down at the empty bucket in her mother's hand and thought, mussels – ugh! "Busy?" she said. "Yes, well, sort of. I'm getting ready to help Papa with the globes."

But just then, Captain Green appeared from around the edge of the huge, ratcheted windlass where he had been busy winding the weights. He wiped the sweat from his forehead, and said, "Hello, Mabel. Do you need Emma? You can take her. There's a bur on the cable I need to take care of – so I won't be ready to polish the globes for a little while."

"Splendid!" said Mrs. Green. "I mean, that's a shame about the bur, but I could use her help," and holding out the bucket, she said to Emma, "Here you are, dear, though you might have to hurry if you want mussels in time for dinner."

 Emma definitely did not want mussels* in time for dinner. But she sighed and came down the ladder anyway to take the bucket from her mother.

She walked across the bridge alone, as Mabel Green remained in the lighthouse talking with her husband. The evening sky was brilliant blue, but punctuated here and there by massive, wet clouds. It was a last remnant of winter, the fragments of a storm that broke up off the coast. There was a trace of winter coolness in the air, but the clouds themselves looked like something Emma might have expected to see during the summer back east – tall thunderheads that climbed nearly to the heavens. Everything was so topsy-turvy here, she reflected, summertime clouds on the tail end of a winter storm.

She walked through the tunnel, up the main path, then turned onto the trail that plunged down the side of the bluff to the cove. As she walked, she hummed to herself and looked this way and that, enjoying the way the light bounced around the clouds and turned everything around her oranger and oranger, in front of her very eyes.

She had almost arrived at the cove when suddenly she thought she heard voices, and she stopped short in order to listen and then stood silently, obscured from the beach by the final bend in the trail. They were definitely voices all right. It took her a moment to recognize them, but eventually she

---

*Saltwater mussels are little "bivalves" – mollusks with two shells. Here in California they grow attached to the rocks, sometimes covering the rock completely. They are edible (some, like my mother, would say delicious, when cooked in white wine and butter) but can be poisonous if you collect them between May and October. *(E.G.)*

realized they belonged to Rascal Pratt, and, just as surprising, to Sue's grandfather, Achilles.

Now, this *is* curious, thought Emma, Achilles down at the cove, and Rascal Pratt actually speaking.

Achilles was very old. No one seemed to know exactly how old he was, but he had worked for the Coles longer than anyone could remember – longer than Harris could remember, longer than Harris's father could remember, and in fact, he supposedly had worked there longer than even Harris's grandfather could remember. According to Sue, he was starting to lose his eyesight. This made him very sad, as it kept him from walking among the hills surrounding the rancho as often as he used to, which was something he was fond of doing. Still, in spite of many years of hard work, he always stood up straight, or maybe leaned a little on his walking stick, and talked in a slow, dignified way, with just a hint of a strange accent.

He was an Indian. But he was not an Indian from California. He was not Miwok or Ohlone – though he had certainly known members of those tribes before so many died, or were killed, or were driven away.* No, Achilles had been brought to California with his mother and father by a Spanish friar when he was just a baby. Not long after that, a

---

*The lands around San Francisco Bay were originally inhabited by two main peoples, the Miwok, who lived north of the bay, where Point Bonita and Sausalito are today, and the Ohlone, who lived south, in what is now San Francisco. Supposedly, it was an area of plenty in those days, with ample food and water, and mild temperatures year round – a real Garden of Eden, and thousands of Miwok and Ohlone lived here! The Miwok and Ohlone are mostly gone now, a result of many tragedies, like diseases brought by Spanish missionaries and American settlers – influenza and small pox for example, and also being forced from their lands and driven from their way of life. *(E.G.)*

strange disease had swept through the Mission of San Rafael, which was not far from Sausalito, and both of his parents died. And now, no one, not even Achilles, knew exactly what part of the Americas he came from. Some said his family was from the Caribbean, while others said Venezuela. But it was all just talk and Achilles himself never spoke of it at all, as it was a painful thing to him. He knew only a few words of his parents' language and otherwise spoke Spanish or English, and he had made a great study of these through the priests at the mission. He was also known as the only one for miles around who could remember any of the old languages of the Indians who had lived on the land around Point Bonita since the times before the Spanish and Americans arrived. And whenever anyone had some question to ask of how things used to be, they came to Achilles.

Emma listened to him speaking now. She always enjoyed the sound of his voice. It was deep and learned, for it was known that he loved studies of any sort, whether it was the wisdom and lore of the original peoples, or the knowledge of the new, which could often be found in books, of which he had collected many since the Mission closed its doors. Also, his voice had a singing quality to it. He left big gaps of silence here and there, even in the middle of sentences, which always gave Emma the impression he was considering deeply whatever he was saying, even if, as was the case now, he was only chatting amiably about the fishing in the area and the collecting of shellfish.

Emma was just about to continue down onto the beach, when she heard Achilles say, "Tell me, young man, if you don't mind, what is that mark on your face?"

Again, Emma stopped dead in her tracks. She was astonished to hear this particular question spoken aloud – anything about a mark on someone's face and, in particular, Rascal Pratt's. It also seemed to astonish Rascal Pratt, since he didn't respond at all.

Achilles spoke again after a second or so. "I'm sorry, I don't mean to pry. And though it may surprise you, I have more than an idle interest in the answer to that question."

There was still more silence from Rascal Pratt. Emma waited for a few minutes, and when she was certain that Rascal Pratt was not going to speak at all on the subject, she decided it was safe to continue innocently round the last bend and into their presence. But then, to her astonishment, she heard Rascal Pratt clear his throat as if he did intend to answer.

"Aye," he said very slowly in his strange lilt, "I know this mark's not pretty to look at, sir, but..." He seemed to pause for another breath and then he said, "Well, I'll tell you, it's punishment for something I once did."

"I see," said Achilles. After a respectful silence he added, "You must know I've heard by now the stories that have been going round since you arrived. So I suppose I should just ask plainly, was it piracy?"

When Emma heard this, she nearly gave herself away with a gasp. For one thing, she was very surprised to hear that any sort of word had 'been going around,' since she was the only one there when Rascal Pratt had said this – at least to her knowledge. Also, she wondered if Rascal Pratt even remembered his feverish rants and, if he did, would he now take Emma to be the blabbermouth who was the source of the rumors that Achilles had heard? She didn't know what to do – to turn around and walk quietly away, or to continue down to the cove as if she had not overheard a thing. As often happens, though, in cases such as these, Emma decided that the best thing to do was simply to quietly stay put, and to listen for just a few seconds more.

At first there was no answer from Rascal Pratt. Emma imagined he was looking at his hands or his feet or at something out in the bay. But certainly, for a long time he did not answer. Eventually though, there came a shuffling of feet and then, as Emma strained to hear, she caught the sound of his voice. He spoke quietly, in the same way Emma would have if she were talking to herself.

"Piracy," the boy mused. "Even if I admitted it, do you think people would actually believe me?"

Achilles chuckled. "My boy, if you are only now asking that question, then I will take the answer to be a simple 'no'. But it's a pity, really, as strangely enough, I find myself requiring the services of a pirate. They are hard to come by these days, you know, and my eyes are growing old. A pirate should have two good eyes no matter what the story books say – or do you think otherwise?"

By this time, Emma almost had to pinch her own arm to convince herself that what she was hearing was not part of a dream. What on earth could Achilles need? And what services could a pirate even provide? Emma could think of nothing but bloody stories, which was completely at odds with Achilles' reputation as a wise and peaceful man. Still, she felt a strange thrill creep up her neck and knew whatever Achilles needed, this was a conversation she should not be overhearing. She was afraid to take a step in any direction, lest she be discovered and she thanked her lucky stars Sammy had not come with her.

On the beach meanwhile, it seemed Achilles had succeeded in whetting Rascal Pratt's curiosity too, for now the boy said in his strangely polite accent, "Tell me, if you will, what is it that you require? Mark on my face or no, I'd be happy to help you however I can."

"No need, no need," said Achilles. "I won't disturb you with it. Anyway, if I'm not mistaken, Emma Green is coming down the trail right this moment. If we don't help her get some mussels for her mother, her family might go hungry. I suppose you could help with that, if you like."

So Emma was found out. Or Achilles had known all along. She blushed and she stepped out around the last bend in the trail and came all the way down to the cove. At the top of the rocky beach she saw Achilles leaning on his walking stick. In his hand he was holding a sack and at his feet were several large abalone*, as well as a crab which was still in a net. "Good evening, Emma," he said.

"Oh, good evening, Achilles," said Emma as innocently as she could. "How did you know I was sent to get mussels?"

"Just a coincidence, I suppose – I've come down to the cove to gather dinner myself – and also to meet this young lad about whom rumors have so much to say."

Rascal Pratt said nothing and only eyed Emma suspiciously. Achilles leaned silently on his stick for a few seconds and then began to gather his abalone as if he were getting ready to leave. As he did, he said, "I got these abalone on that rock over there when the tide was out. You know which rock I mean – that boulder at the foot of the cliff. It's interesting, the Indians here before us had names for all these rocks we see. The whites, too, named a few. The abalone rock for instance –the whites have always called it 'Keg Rock," and

---

*The abalone is a large mollusk which is eight to twelve inches across. It clings to rocks and can be found at the tide line and in much deeper waters. It is prized as food. It has a beautiful, round shell, which becomes a beautiful iridescent when it, unfortunately, dies. *(E.G.)*

that one way out across the water is of course 'Mile Rock.' It's very famous. But those are not names, no more than *Achilles* is. Really, those are *re*names, if you know what I mean, names which men make do in a pinch. But the people before us had other names for the rocks, because the rocks still had spirits of their own. The ancient names were ones like *Anna-babe-at-the-sea*, though of course it wasn't really Anna, it was an Indian name that I shan't disrespect by saying aloud, and others like *Belle-the-whisker-rake*."

Achilles bent down to pick up another abalone. As he did, he went on. "Anyway, here's a strange thing, there's another rock not too far from here, a few miles north of the point. But of all the rocks and all the names, the Indians *never* called that one in their own language. They used an English name." He looked at Emma and Rascal Pratt meaningfully. "I always found that to be curious myself, since this was when I was just a boy, and long before any English-speaking settlers got here – why this was back in the Spanish days. And it made me wonder of course where that name came from. An English name, used by the Indians, even before English-speakers arrived – it's odd, isn't it? No one has used that name for a long time now. I remember it though. As I recall, that rock was always called *The Pretty Red*."

At this, Rascal Pratt suddenly stood up straight in his crutches. He did it so quickly that the change in weight almost made him slip. Emma looked over to him, but he turned quickly away.

Achilles evidently found something humorous in this and he chuckled aloud. He turned to face the sea one last time, as though to take a deep breath of the wind that came off it. "Yes, that's what they called it, *The Pretty Red*," he said. "Don't you like that name? I certainly do."

The Mystery of Rascal Pratt

- 6 -

The Boat Works

After that, Achilles began to show up at the cove at Point Bonita several times a week. He would make the trip whenever Sue and Harris came to visit Emma. Emma was amazed at how fast the old man walked, in spite of his age and his eyesight. Harris and Sue would stop at the Green's house, but Achilles, who usually beat them by a few minutes, always went directly down to the cove. And at first, Rascal Pratt would leave the house right after him, hobbling down to the cove on his crutches, the minute he saw Achilles walking by.

But as time went on, Emma noticed that Rascal Pratt began to linger downstairs a little longer each morning, even though Achilles had walked by the house already. Until then, Rascal Pratt had hardly said a thing other than perhaps to grunt "G'morning" or to utter a word of thanks for his breakfast – and this only to Mrs. Green and no one else. But when Harris and Sue – especially Sue – walked into the room, his face would brighten in a way that was obvious. Still, he seldom spoke and he would eventually take his leave to join Achilles at the cove after a time. But each day, his visits with the other children got a little longer. This was quite a change, since before, aside from his size, it would have been hard to say for certain that he was a child at all. He was far more serious than Emma or Harris or Sue, and in fact, whenever they laughed at any sort of joke, he frowned and look away with some impatience. Still, there he was, each day hovering a little longer on the outside of their circle.

Down at the cove, it turned out, Achilles was helping Rascal Pratt fix his dory – the little boat in which he had drifted into their lives several weeks before. Achilles often brought with him pieces of wood that he thought might work well in a particular part of the repair, like a knee from an apple tree to use as a thwart. But then, after it was plain that Rascal Pratt was making steady progress, Achilles stopped bringing wood and started showing up with bundles of reeds tied to the back of a little donkey. Sue told Emma that Achilles collected the reeds very carefully from a marsh on the north side of the hill, and soon it became clear that Achilles was also working on a boat of his own. It was a reed boat. He said it was a design he had learned from the Miwok when he was just a child.* Harris, Sue, and Emma all took great interest in the work on both boats, and even Captain and Mrs. Green began to make trips down to the little boatyard that had sprung up in the cove.

One day Emma, Harris, and Sue were watching Achilles put the finishing touches on his boat, when Captain Green came to visit. For a while he admired the work of Achilles' boat and asked a question or two, which Achilles answered politely, though never with too many words. He might even have asked some more questions had not Achilles excused himself, saying it was time for him to return to the rancho.

Captain Green then came over to inspect Rascal Pratt's dory. He seemed almost startled to see the progress the boy had made – or so Emma thought. She saw how her father looked east, across the bay towards San  Francisco, and even pulled out his pocket watch absentmindedly, almost as though he were expecting someone to arrive that very day.

"Are you planning a trip, Mr. Pratt?" he inquired. "Your leg's not mended and the water here may be more dangerous than you're used to, you know."

Emma had long before noticed that Rascal Pratt never spoke to her father if he could avoid it and instead only looked at the ground or floor if the captain spoke to him. The same was true this day. Though Captain Green had addressed

---

*The Miwok Indians, who lived on the shores of the San Francisco Bay, made reed boats which they called "sakas." They were used to travel across the bay and into the rivers and estuaries. They varied in size. Some were built to carry just one hunter or fisherman; others were large enough to transport several people and heavy loads of cargo. (E.G.)

him directly, Rascal Pratt didn't answer and only continued with his work, as though his host – for that was in fact what Captain Green was to him – hadn't spoken to him at all. At length, Captain Green shrugged, bid everyone a good day and left the cove. But as he did, Emma saw Rascal Pratt lift his eyes and watch her father until he had disappeared up the trail. Rascal Pratt happened to glance over to Emma too and realized that Emma was watching him. He went a little crimson in the face, but instead of appearing embarrassed, he blurted almost angrily, "You people act as though you've never been in a boat before. Why are you all so afraid of the water?"

"Well, the water is dangerous," said Emma matter-of-factly. She was merely repeating what she believed and what she had been told many times.

"Of course it's dangerous," said Rascal Pratt. "But it's all around you here. You can't avoid it forever, you know. And your own father a *sea captain!*"

"Well, I'm not afraid of the water," Harris put in just then. He was sitting with Sue and Emma in a patch of yellow verbena*. "I saved you from it, after all."

Rascal Pratt snorted. "You?" he said. "Saved me? Why, if you hadn't pulled me into this cove, I'd have bumped and lumped on the tide all the way to Sausalito. I'm just sorry you didn't let me go by."

"I am too," said Harris. "Your boat would've sunk and

---

*Verbena is a little flowering plant with pink and yellow varieties and lives among the dunes, sometimes in the desert, and sometimes near the sea. It's very pretty and has fuzzy stems that collect sand right out of the wind. The sand then collects water and also helps protect it from the harsh environment near the ocean. *(E.G.)*

you'd have drowned."

"Is that right?" said Rascal Pratt. "I'll have you know that little boat made it here from—" but before he finished what he was going to say, he stopped himself.

The other three – Harris, Sue, and Emma – looked at him all the more closely.

"Well, from where?" said Harris. "Where'd you come from then, in that little boat? Why, your boat looks more like a child's boat than a pirate's. Admit it, you aren't really a pirate!"

Rascal Pratt cast a glance toward Emma and Sue, and after a second or two said coolly, "I'm not in the habit of boasting, but since you press me like this, I'll admit it: I am. No need though to spread the word around."

Harris, however, only laughed. "There's nothing to spread around! The days of piracy are long over. You're only about a hundred and fifty years too late."

"What would you like, for me to tell you some old pirating tales?" said Rascal Pratt, "Well *I* don't kiss and tell. Besides, what I know, I *have* to keep secret."

"Sure, either that, or you don't have anything to keep secret to begin with," said Harris.

"Yes, Mr. Cole, you're right, " Rascal Pratt said sarcastically. "In fact, I branded my face with a hot iron just to keep up with the fashions – everyone knows how the ladies just love a man with a brand. If you want to get married, I really recommend getting one, right on your face, where everyone can see it!"

No one said anything for a few minutes, until finally Sue spoke. "How... how did you get that brand, Rascal Pratt?" she asked gently. "If you got caught, and I guess you did, then that story can't be a secret."

Rascal Pratt's eyes darted around the little group. Then a sly smile spread across his face, as though an idea had just come to him, and he said almost jovially, "No red-blooded pirate likes to tell the tale of his own downfall, but since you probably read all about it in the newspapers already, I don't suppose it would hurt to tell my side." And with that, he sat on a driftwood log, laying his crutches beside him. He propped his elbows on his knees and began to tell his tale. Everything about him changed – his voice, his way of talking. He lifted his eyes upward, looking past his audience and toward the sky and bluffs behind them, as though he were trying to compose the exact details of the story in his own mind.

"I was hove-to, so to speak, in the city of Balboa, on the Pacific coast of Panama, you see. I was with my brother at the time. We'd just left the crew of the famous Captain... Captain Gunsword Whetcutt. You've all heard of him, of course – now don't say you haven't! Well, we were living it up at the Hotel... the Hotel Christobal, the way crew members do. The weather was as hot and muggy as you can imagine, and one night it was downright *insufferable*. There weren't a puff of air, and my brother and myself, neither of us could sleep, so we decided to walk down to the wharf, to see if it wasn't a bit cooler by the water. Now while we were down there, my brother says to me, 'I'm about ready to be moving on, Rascal Pratt,' and I, of course, says, 'Aye', like I usually did, on account of he being older than me. But Captain Whetcutt's ship had long left and, as Mr. Cole has already pointed out, pirate ships are few and far between these days. So we thought we'd have to sign up onboard another ship, as merchantmen. Regular merchantmen – sailors on a cargo ship! One thing you must know – and if you don't, then I won't tell anymore of this story – is that pirates loathe good, honest work, as they loathe everything wholesome. So the prospect of a three-month voyage before the mast and under the heel of a task-master of a sea captain, chipping and painting – I can tell you *that* had very little appeal.

"Now as it happened, lying there at the wharf, as pretty as a picture, was an ocean-going yawl, not too different from a Gloucester fisher, only a little lower in the water and no doubt a lot faster. As we walked by it, my brother looked at me and I looked at him. It didn't seem there was a single soul on board. The boat was only forty-five feet or so in length, just a baby of a ship really, and we knew right then and there that we had found our ticket out of Panama.

"So, I ran back to the room as quick as I could to collect our belongings and my brother stayed to watch over the ship, our ship. But when I got to the hotel, it was clear there was some sort of police action unfolding. A whole squad of Panamanian soldiers was standing outside at the fountain. Oh, they had the prettiest uniforms – red, with gold epaulets. The least private had an ostrich feather in his cap, and most were engaged in waving to ladies looking down from various windows around the square. Just then, as I'm walking into the front door, I hear someone say, in Spanish of course, 'There he is, right there, one of the Pratt brothers.' Until that moment, I never realized I was famous -- though I supposed sailing with Whetcutt Gunsword, that's commonplace. Anyway, the captain of the platoon stamps and all the soldiers commence to chasing me. There was nowhere to run but into the

hotel, and from there, into the casino. I was darting this way
and that. Luckily, I had on my richest suit of clothing so no
one looked at me sideways. I had gotten to the back without
getting caught and had found the gentlemen's lounge, where
I was just trying to slip out the windows. But then, by good
luck or bad, you tell me, I overheard a certain conversation.

"I heard Yankee accents, which is not so unusual and so
I would have ignored it altogether, except one fellow said to
another, 'Well, you'll have to come visit us on our yawl. She's
brand new, her masts were hewn from the tallest forest in the
whole state of Maine, and she's faster than any sailing vessel
I've ever been on. She's a thoroughbred, I tell you, and she's
down at the pier right now. But, my wife and baby daughter
are asleep onboard, so come by tomorrow, not tonight.'

"Of course, I stopped and turned to see who was talking,
and I'll be a monkey's uncle if it wasn't an officer in the U.S.
Navy. He was an admiral no doubt – or a commodore, even
– they're all the same to me. Anyway, it now seemed the case,
plain and simple, that my brother and I were planning to
make off with the private yacht of an officer in the U.S. Navy,
and not only that, we were probably kidnapping an innocent
woman and child in the bargain. I had to warn my brother!
As soon as the men left the room, I leapt from the bathroom
window. And would you believe it? – I landed all wrong! I
was aiming for a wagon already hitched up with horses, but
I bounced from the seat and crashed onto the cobblestones.
In fact, I broke my leg! Yes, that's right, I did, and it never did
set right – that's certainly one reason it broke so easily again.

"Well, anyway, I got down to the wharf as fast as I could,
which considering I was practically dragging one leg along
behind me, wasn't too terribly fast and, all the while, my
brother waiting for me. My brother! Now, he's not known

for his patience – few pirates are. And so when I get there, I see to my distress that he has already climbed aboard the yawl, untied her, and is holding her against the pier with his foot and one line 'round a cleat.

" 'Where's our loot?' says he when he sees me returning empty handed, since we had left a largish share of coin and pretty jewels back at the hotel.

" 'Brother, you must get off the boat!' says I, as quietly as I could.

" 'Where's our loot?' he says again, louder this time.

"And again I say, 'We must not take that boat!' Only just then, as luck would have it, the platoon of soldiers arrives at the wharf, making an awful hullabaloo. I stepped onto the yawl to explain to my brother as expediently as I could why we should leave the boat alone, but what does he do but cast off? The current grabs hold of us and takes us into the little harbor! Oh, he's a fiend for escapes, my brother is, and he could get a boat out of any pinch. And admiring his handy work, the wharf getting farther and farther away in the inky stillness of the night, he turns to me with a grin as big and proud as a Cheshire cat's and says, 'What's that you say?' Oh yes, he was a fiend for escapes and close shaves.

"But this time, we would have been better off jumping into the harbor ourselves and swimming out with the tide, rich suits and all. I tried my best to grab hold of the wharf, to stop us, but I could not.

" 'Dear brother,' I cried, 'we're undone! There's a lady aboard this ship, and her baby too – the wife and child of an American naval officer. We're doomed if we take this vessel. We're doomed already, for we're adrift and we have no wind to return the lady and the child even if we wanted.'

"My poor brother's smile drooped, neither of us would

kidnap a lady and her child on purpose, as there are strict rules against just this thing, and hardly taking time to think of himself, my brother says, 'Well, there must be a guard aboard then too, probably asleep. We'll wake him. But, brother, we must be careful – let's not get shot.' "

Rascal Pratt had apparently come to the end of his tale. His last words, he spoke more softly than the rest. Emma was astonished at the change that had come over him as he remembered fonder days. She knew if she said the smallest thing she would break the spell, but she couldn't help herself as she asked, "So, what happened?"

Rascal Pratt looked up at her. He seemed very far way. He shrugged and said, "We woke the guard, a young midshipman actually, and with a mighty heave of the anchor, the three of us managed to catch hold of the breakwater at the harbor entrance. We bade the midshipman to arrest us, rather than take our chances with the soldiers. The U.S. Navy was good enough to bring us here – back to the States, that is."

A cloud flitted across the sun and the cove briefly fell into shadow. The color that the story had returned to Rascal Pratt's face seemed to fade again. He stirred and, seeing that everyone was watching him, he self-consciously touched the scar on his cheek and looked away.

The two girls seemed completely impressed with the tale; that's certainly how Emma felt. But – and maybe because of this – Harris said, "Well, if that's really the way it happened, you can't count it as piracy."

Rascal Pratt didn't look at Harris. He answered wearily, still looking out over the cove, "And why is that, Mr. Cole?"

"Because it's just stealing," said Harris.

"But Harris," said Emma, "don't you see, he took the boat back, to avoid the greater crime of kidnapping."

"Yes, but I'm talking about *piracy*," said Harris. "Piracy is when you take another ship at sea, with force – and a cutlass. This is just common theft."

"Common?" said Rascal Pratt suddenly, pulling himself out of his trance. He spun around, and with surprising speed he had his crutches under his arms and was standing over them. "Are you saying I'm a common thief?"

"No," said Harris, standing himself, "I'm trying to help you – if that's the story you're going to tell. You should be careful because that's how you paint yourself, as a thief, not a pirate."

Rascal Pratt drew an arm back, but stopped short of striking Harris, as Emma had suddenly feared he intended to do. He looked at the other boy for a long time and at length said, "You know, it's you who should be careful who you call a thief. It's you after all who's living on lands you stole from people like Miss Hermanastra here, and Achilles, and now you treat them like servants."

This comment came completely out of the blue and it seemed to surprise and confuse everyone, certainly Emma – and Harris much more so. Before Harris could say anything though, Sue jumped between the two boys.

"Stop, both of you!" she said, and to Harris she added, "I don't know what's the matter with you, but I really liked Rascal Pratt's story. I asked him to tell it." Then she turned to scold Rascal Pratt, though she ended up saying nothing and instead shot him an icy look which Emma happened to catch as well.

If Sue's look had meant for Rascal Pratt to keep quiet, as Emma suspected it did, it only agitated him further, and he said, "What a mistake it was to waste a story on you. Do you think such stories, the tales of other folk's misfortunes, are spun just for your amusement? I should have known, young *Master* Cole, son of Edgar Cole, and soon to be following in his father's footsteps! You, who don't know the first thing about boats or water, telling me who's a pirate and who's a mere thief!" He now seemed angry at them all, at least at Harris and Emma, and pointing to them he said, "Twelve years old and you don't even know how to swim. You know, Achilles says Indian children a lot younger than you paddled their reed boats way out onto the bay to gather bird eggs from the rocks—"

But Sue wouldn't let him finish. "Stop, Rascal Pratt. Don't you dare bring my grandfather into this. He's an old man and I think he deserves some amount of peace before he dies. If you can't say anything nice about my friends, don't say anything at all. After all, they've only helped you."

"They haven't helped me. They're just a couple of—"

"I said, *stop!*" exclaimed Sue.

Rascal Pratt's eyes flashed angrily. It was almost as if Sue, in preventing him from getting satisfaction from Harris, had plainly betrayed him. He looked sullenly away.

Harris however waved his hand and said, "Hey, Sue, it's all right, I... I guess I did sorta start it. Rascal Pratt, listen, let's just forget it, I shouldn't have... you know." He stopped short of actually apologizing. Rascal Pratt said nothing and stood with his back turned.

Harris shrugged. "All right, suit yourself," he said to Rascal Pratt. And to the others he added, "I have to leave anyway. I gotta get home before my pa starts to think I'm trying to get out of my chores."

"Take your friends with you," Rascal Pratt muttered, still facing the other way. At this, Emma got up slowly, assuming that Rascal Pratt meant her as well. She was bewildered that it had all come to this. She watched Harris walking up the trail and she turned to look at Rascal Pratt. His back was still turned, but she could see enough of him to see his face was scarlet with rage and his scar stood out a livid white.

"Goodbye, Rascal Pratt," she said softly. "I liked your story too." She didn't expect him to answer. He didn't. She sighed, dusted her dress, and turned to leave with Harris. To her surprise Sue stood to join her.

When Rascal Pratt noticed this, he spat. "You're going with them?"

"Of course," Sue shot back, "as you said yourself, they *are* my friends." Then she turned and hurried to catch up with Harris and Emma before they reached the trail.

No sooner were they all out of earshot from Rascal Pratt, than Harris muttered, "I'm telling you, there's something's fishy about him. And if he's sixteen, I'll... I'll be a monkey's uncle too. Why, I'm twelve and I'm bigger than him. Stronger than him too, I bet. Next mystery to solve – the Mystery of Rascal—"

"Oh, please don't, Harris," interrupted Sue. "I was hoping we wouldn't talk about him behind his back. He's odd, I agree, but he's a friend too. And I know my grandfather has become very fond of him. I just don't think we should..."

"Well, we should what?" said Harris impatiently when Sue didn't finish her sentence.

"I don't think we should treat him as a *mystery*, not that sort of mystery, anyway. You can be a mystery too, you know, but I don't exactly want to *solve* you."

This struck all three of them as funny and they all began to laugh, though probably none of them could have said exactly why.

"So Rascal Pratt's really your friend then?" said Harris to

Sue through his chuckles.

"Well, of course," said Sue.

"Mine too," Emma piped up, even if no one had really asked her.

Harris paused for a moment on the trail. The girls continued walking. He shook his head, then trotted a few steps to catch up again. And as he did, he said, "Well, look, I never said I *didn't* like him."

- 7 -
Drake's Bay

A few evenings later, Emma was in the lighthouse, helping her father. The sun was still an inch or so above the horizon. It was a big, orange ball ready to drop into the sea, which for once was perfectly flat. Not a puff of wind rippled the ocean surface, while far away, in the opposite side of the sky, a full moon was just poking over the hills, a big, flat disk the color of a lemon. Aside from a single harrier*, which floated up and down at the edge of the bluff, nothing outside the lantern room moved. It was as though the whole world had stopped in respect of the changing of the guard, as the moon relieved the sun in its labors across the sky.

Emma too stopped what she was doing to admire the quiet end of the day. Before she resumed her task, she happened to notice a movement on the water directly below the lighthouse. It seemed a little boat had come around the point and was now skirting the cliffs so closely that it was nearly impossible to see. Emma recognized the boat immediately and she recognized the rower in it. It was Rascal Pratt, of course.

She glanced up at her father. He hadn't yet seen the boat. He was frowning just then as he inspected the job he had done on the wicks.

"I'm all done with the globes, Papa," she said.

"Very good," said the captain. "I'm not quite done with these wicks – but if you like, you can go up to the house and help your mother with supper. Or you can wait for me. I'll be just a few more minutes."

"Oh, I'm in no hurry," said Emma, "I'll wait outside."

She slid down the ladder to the watch-room and pushed open the door to step out onto the platform that surrounded it. She leaned forward to look over the edge of the cliff. By

---

*The harrier is a small bird of prey, much smaller than the redtail hawks that are so common here. There is a young harrier that I see around Point Bonita quite often. My mother says it's a young one (a *juvenile*). Its hunting technique is really something – it hovers over the very crest of a hill or at the edge of bluffs, perfectly still, without a single wing-beat. *(E.G.)*

then Rascal Pratt was almost below her, steadily dipping his oars in the water, stroke after stroke. For a second, Emma was afraid he was leaving them. As she watched, he disappeared around the next point of rock. Then it occurred to her that if he really were leaving, he would have taken something with him on his journey, even if just a meal wrapped in oiled paper. But the dory had been empty, aside from the boy and his oars. And indeed, not more than a minute later, he reappeared from around the point and began rowing back. One thing was for certain: however old he really was, he was quite a speedy rower.

Later that evening, at supper, as her mother and father chatted about the various parts of the day, Emma chewed her food quietly. It wasn't until they were midway through the meal that either parent seemed to notice Emma had hardly said a word, and her mother asked, "Deep in thought, dear?"

Emma started and looked up. "Oh," she said, "yes, I suppose. I was just thinking – do the words 'Pretty Red' mean anything to you?"

Mrs. Green shrugged. "Pretty red what?"

"Just Pretty Red," said Emma. "That's all, *the* Pretty Red, maybe?"

"No," said Mrs. Green, "it doesn't mean anything to me."

But Captain Green wiped his mouth on his napkin and asked, "Is it 'pretty red'? Or '*the* pretty red'? As I recall, *the Pretty Red* was the name of the flag used by the English privateers. When French sailors saw it, they would sing out the warning, '*le jolie rouge!*' *Le jolie rouge* means *the pretty red*. It's where we get the name the Jolly Roger. See – *Jolie Rouge* – Jolly Roger. They weren't always skull and cross bones you know, just a red flag with a simple design in the center. When they flew it, it meant 'we give no quarter', which is another way of saying, 'Surrender, or we'll murder every last one of you!'"

"John!" Mrs. Green protested.

"Well, pirating wasn't exactly a pretty business, Mabel, as much as we like to romanticize it, from the safe distance of a hundred and fifty years. Anyway, where did you hear it, Emma?"

"Oh, I don't know," said Emma, "down in the cove. One of the kids, I guess."

Captain Green smiled. "Ah yes, someone has been reading about Sir Francis Drake, no doubt! Great stories, those. I loved them as a kid myself. Some people say Drake landed near here, you know. That's why we have Drake's Bay, just on the other side of the point. If Drake was here, it was long ago, even before the Spanish made it this far north. According to his logs, he had taken a couple of Spanish treasure ships not long before and he stopped here to repair his boat. They say he left a metal disk and a few other things. No one has ever found them."

Emma thought about this for a moment, and then said, "What's a privateer?"

"Well, a privateer is like a pirate, only he worked for his country," said Captain Green. "He would give his treasure to the king or queen that he worked for. And of course he got to keep some himself. Drake was the most famous privateer of all – perhaps the finest seaman who ever lived. He got enormously wealthy on all the gold he took."

Emma put her fork down and, more thinking aloud than speaking, she said, "So there *were* pirates here."

"Privateers, dear," said Captain Green. "Pirates were

scoundrels. Rapscallions. But privateers were heroes, officers of the royal navy, amassing glory for the crown."

"But they both attacked unsuspecting ships, didn't they? And stole treasure? And maybe even buried it?"

Captain Green laughed. "I don't know about burying it, though I suppose they might have. I can imagine that not every member of Drake's crew was so happy to give all that treasure back to the queen. In those days, a handful of gold coins was more than a sailor could make in a lifetime."

"A whole lifetime?" repeated Emma in awe.

Before Captain Green could answer, there was a *clump, clump, clump* up the back steps. The door opened, and who should step into the kitchen but Rascal Pratt. When he saw the family eating, he rested for a second, leaning on his crutches.

"Well, speaking of rapscallions!" said Mrs. Green in the kindly voice she always used when she addressed the boy, "it's Master Pratt himself."

Rascal Pratt smiled shyly and looked at the floor.

"Working late on your boat, eh, Mr. Pratt?" said Captain Green in the stiff tone he always used when he addressed the boy.

"Indeed, sir," said Rascal Pratt in the funny lilt he always used when he addressed anybody. "She's as good as new I'd say. Just took her for a row in fact – around the point. She handles nicely."

"In the dark?" said Captain Green, as he looked suspiciously at the boy. "Not very prudent, Mr. Pratt."

"Well, sir, I was back in the cove before the pink was out of the sky. T'is a pretty evening to be on the water, sir."

"All the same," said the captain, "it's too late. I don't want to have to pluck you off one of the rocks. Do you understand?"

Rascal Pratt looked up from the floor and squinted at the captain. It was clear to Emma that he disliked being addressed this way, and he said politely, but also in a way that seemed like a challenge, "Yes, I understand, sir. Of course, you're welcome to take her out yourself. I recommend it. But only if you feel up to it. These waters are tricky, you're right about that. Rowing in the mouth of this bay is not for everyone, I admit."

At this, Mrs. Green rapidly cut in, before her husband had an opportunity to respond. "Well, ah, Mr. Pratt, you must be hungry. Perhaps you care for supper?"

The next morning, Captain Green was leaving the lighthouse for two days. He was going to Sausalito, then to San Francisco, on official Lighthouse Service business. It was to be his first trip back to the city since the Green family had moved to Point Bonita. Emma and her mother were going to keep the lighthouse for him. Mostly it would be Emma's job. Captain Green even gave her a rank in the Lighthouse Service, naming her Assistant Lighthouse Keeper, Point Bonita, First Officer of the Watch. In the evenings she was to light the lantern and set the machinery in motion and in the mornings she was to do just the opposite. During the day, she was to perform all the routine maintenance, like making sure there was plenty of fuel for the light and making certain all the machinery, not to mention the lens, was shipshape. There was plenty to do and, on top of it all, when she wasn't busy, she was to sit at the desk in the watch-room to note the ships that came in and out of the bay, recording in the log the comings and goings of anything with more than one mast.

So, sit she did. The next day, after she finished her work

with the lens and the machinery, she sat with her father's spyglass in her hand, the massive logbook open in front of her, standing watch now, not just over the lighthouse, but the entrance of the whole bay. The day though was just as still as the one before, not a day for sailing, and by the middle of the morning, she had yet to see a single boat. She wished she had brought a book. She turned the spyglass onto the birds, the seals, the rocks. As she did, she could not help but wonder which was the one Achilles had called "the Pretty Red."

After a while, Sammy, who was lying at her feet, lifted his head and barked. Emma looked out the window and saw Sue and Harris making their way across the footbridge. Thank goodness, she thought, company!

"Hello, Emma!" called Sue as she climbed up the ladder to the lantern room. "Your mother said we'd find you out here at the light."

"Hello, hello!" Emma said in return. "You're just in time for lunch."

Sue looked out the window and up at the sun in the sky. "So early?"

"Well, mostly I'm bored," admitted Emma. "But, *you* must be hungry – it's a long walk from your house."

Sue shook her head "no." Harris, however, said, "I am. What you got there?"

So Emma unwrapped the food she had carried out from the house, happy to have someone to share it with. As she did, she remembered what she had learned the night before at the dinner table... and so she told her friends what her father had said about the Pretty Red, the Jolly Roger, and also about Sir Francis Drake.

"So," said Sue, musing slowly, "he *is* a pirate, then."

"Rascal Pratt?" said Emma. "A pirate? Nowadays? Maybe

he just read how they called the flag the Pretty Red in a book or something."

Sue frowned, but nodded anyway, saying, "Sure. Maybe."

"Hey," said Harris, who until then had been contentedly munching on a piece of bread and butter, "that reminds me – as we were coming over the bluff, I saw Rascal Pratt. He was walking out of your barn, carrying tools – at least a shovel. I waved, but he didn't wave back. I think he's still angry with me. But, do you suppose he's going on a treasure hunt?"

"Certainly not to the Pretty Red," said Sue, "He can't get there without a boat."

"But, he does have a boat!" Emma exclaimed. "I saw him rowing last night. He finished his repairs!"

Harris looked at Sue. Sue looked at Emma. Emma looked at Harris. And they each jumped for the ladder, as though they all had the same idea, at the same time, of rushing down to the cove.

"But wait," said Harris to Emma suddenly, putting out his arm and stopping the others, "aren't you on duty here?"

Emma stopped and glanced around the lantern room. The spyglass sat quietly on the desk. The log was open to a clean page. Outside, the air and water were perfectly still. Emma waved her hand. "No wind," she said, "No ships today. Let's go!"

They slid down the ladder, taking care to hand Sammy down too, then ran out of the lighthouse and back across the bridge. They ran through the tunnel, up the steep hill, and down the trail to the cove. They were all out of breath by the time they reached the beach. But when they got there, they realized they were too late. Rascal Pratt's boat was gone.

"He left already!" moaned Emma. "How long ago did

you see him, Harris?"

"Not long, just before we saw you. He can't have gotten too far. After all, he had to push his boat down to the water, and with a broken leg."

"Or, maybe without a broken leg," said Sue, who at that moment was inspecting a clump of kelp where the anchor to Rascal Pratt's boat used to be. "Don't you recognize these?" She turned over the kelp with her foot. On the beach lay a pair of crutches.

"Why, that... that rapscallion!" cried Emma. "My poor mama's been carrying food to him for weeks!"

"A rapscallion, hey?" said Harris with a teasing smile. "Well, don't say I never warned you."

"All right, so you did. Well, if we had stayed in the light-house, we'd at least have seen him come around the point. Come on, let's go back and see if we can see him now."

She and Harris were starting to leave the beach, when from behind them, closer to the water, Sue said, "Stop. Let's follow him." Emma turned to look. There was a strange, determined look in Sue's eye.

"How can we follow him?" said Emma. "We can't follow him from shore – in most places, we can't even get to the edge of the cliffs."

"Well, what about Achilles' reed boat?" Sue suggested. "I think it's finished."

At this, Emma cried out, "Oh, no!" She hadn't meant to sound so alarmed, but she had no desire to go anywhere by water. More calmly, she added, "I mean, we don't know the first thing about boats."

"I do," Harris said indignantly. "Rascal Pratt's not the only one who knows about boats, you know."

Sue added, "We can always turn back at the edge of the

cove." She walked over to the reed boat and picked it up by its bow. "Look, it's as light as a feather. And remember what Rascal Pratt said – even children could handle these and took them out to the rocks looking for bird eggs."

But this did not make Emma feel any safer. She looked at the boat mistrustfully and then back out over the bay. The sun danced playfully off the water. Even the cliffs way over on the San Francisco side of the Golden Gate seemed friendly and almost close by. It all looked like a big, flat pond; in fact, it was hard to believe it was one of the most dangerous stretches of water in the whole world. Emma took a deep breath. "I suppose it's calm, at least. All right, I'll go with you. But first sign of danger, can you promise we'll turn around?"

Sue and Harris agreed.

"Sammy, stay here, then." said Emma. She, Harris and Sue picked up the boat from the beach and walked it down to the water's edge where they set it down again in the shallows. Sammy followed them, of course.

Sue and Emma took off their shoes and placed them in the boat. Harris, on the other hand, kept his on. "I don't intend to get wet," he said with a professional air. But no sooner had he said this than a small wave broke on the beach and drenched his feet up to the ankles. The girls giggled. At first Harris shot them an irritated glance, but then laughing at himself, said, "On the other hand, I suppose if you're going to fool around with boats, you've got to get your feet wet!"

Harris and Sue let Emma get into the boat first. It rocked as she stepped in. Her stomach immediately felt queasy even though the water there at the beach's edge was hardly a foot deep. Emma closed her eyes, took another breath, and did her best to quiet her nerves. It's going to be all right, she told herself, Harris and Sue know what they're doing. Meanwhile however, Sammy whimpered uneasily and dashed about in shallow water. Emma consoled him. "It – it'll be fine. Really, Sammy. Fine." And she hoped it would be.

Sue climbed into the bow, and Harris, in his wet shoes, waded them out a few feet to deeper water before hopping into the stern. There was only one paddle. Sue took it, as it was already in the bow. It had blades on both ends, like an Inuit paddle, and each blade was pointed. She dipped one blade in the water, then the other. Emma looked back at the shore. They were moving, gliding gracefully along. Sammy barked one final time, then retreated up the path, away from beach, as though he couldn't bear to watch. Silly dog, thought Emma. This is easy. And indeed, in almost no time at all, they were at the edge of the cove.

"So how does it look?" asked Emma, trying to peer around the corner of rock and into the open sea beyond.

"Calm," said Sue. She rested the paddle across her knees. "Though I don't see Rascal Pratt. Where do you suppose he disappeared to?"

All three of them craned their necks to see around the point, but the water beyond them was empty of any sort of vessel, large or small, for as far as they could see. Their reed boat edged farther away from shore and farther out of the cove. "Harris, stop paddling," said Sue.

"I'm not paddling," said Harris. "I don't have a paddle, remember?"

Emma and Sue swiveled around to look. Sure enough, Harris was only sitting in the back of the boat, his hands folded in his lap.

To one side, on the right hand, was the rock wall where the foot of Point Bonita came down to the water. To their left was the Golden Gate, the mouth of San Francisco Bay. And straight ahead was the Pacific Ocean. From the vastness of the ocean alone, it would have been hard to judge if they were actually moving, but there on their right, the rock wall continued to slide silently past. Yes, they were moving, all right.

"Oh no!" Sue cried, "We've drifted out too far – the current's got us!"

Emma twisted this way and that, looking in every direction for help, any help at all. She happened to look up and there, high above them on the cliff, she saw the lighthouse, Point Bonita Light, the last line of coastal defense. But it looked completely empty. It *was* completely empty. After all, today was the day she was officer of the watch.

- 8 -

The Potato Patch

Sue paddled backward with all her might. In the stern, Harris paddled with his hands. Emma thought she should at least try to help. She leaned uncertainly over the side and took a feeble swipe or two at the water. It was obvious, though, that it was all in vain; the current was simply too strong. The cove, the point, the lighthouse – they all just got farther and farther away.

By this time, they were already a hundred yards from shore. To Emma, this might as well have been a thousand, as a hundred yards over water, no matter how calm, was something she just couldn't cross. She remembered the warnings from her first days at Point Bonita, about how she risked getting swept over the horizon if she so much as got into a boat; and, now, seeing this really coming true, how the horizon really did appear to pull them towards it, she was overcome with distress. She began to scream frantically for help.

"Mama!" she shouted hysterically. She stood and shouted in all directions, "Anyone! Help! HELP!" causing the boat to tip dangerously from side to side.

"Emma, don't!" exclaimed Harris, reaching forward and trying to stop her. "If Captain Green finds us, he'll tan our hides!"

Emma blinked dumbly at Harris. Then she turned back towards land and shouted louder than ever, "Help! Mother! HHELLLPPP!" When she could shout no more, she sat down forlornly. "Captain Green won't tan anyone's hide today – he went to San Francisco, remember?"

At that moment Sue said in an odd voice, "Hey, you two – are the waves getting bigger? Or is that my imagination?"

Emma looked out to sea, to where Sue was pointing. A large wave, strangely large for such a calm day, was breaking another hundred yards beyond them, in a place she had heard her father call the Potato Patch*. No one knew the exact rea-

---

*The Potato Patch, also called Four Fathom Bank, stretches west, just off Point Bonita. Its exact boundaries move around a little each winter. It's mostly a sand shoal and is dangerous chiefly for the waves it produces, and close to Point Bonita, just east of the Bonita Channel, I've also seen many hazardous rocks. (E.G.)

son why it was called this. Some people said a boat full of farm produce had wrecked there once and left the water full of potatoes. Others said the strange currents running every which-way when the whole of San Francisco Bay tried to return to the sea via the narrow mouth of the Golden Gate made the water boil, like a kettle of potatoes on the stove. In any case, the Potato Patch was a dangerous, underwater shoal of sandbars and boulders at the entrance of the bay. It had claimed many a seagoing vessel. And now the current was dragging Emma and her friends directly towards it.

"That's a big wave, all right," Emma heard Harris say in a low, serious voice. "Hang onto your hats, everyone!"

The wave was starting to rear itself up into a wall as it moved over the shallowest part of the shoal. As it approached, it rose higher and higher. Emma closed her eyes. Her stomach dropped as she felt their little craft rise into the air. But, for whatever reason, perhaps a million of them, the wave never quite broke. It lifted them up, up, up, and then, it set them gently back down as it rolled harmlessly under them and into the deeper water of the channel.

"Oh... my...," said Emma as she opened her eyes and clutched her stomach. She was nearly as green as the sea itself, and she groaned, "Could we please, *please* not do that again?"

No one answered, but Sue pointed out to sea with her paddle. Another wave was starting to push itself up into a mountain of moving water. It was much larger than the one before it, and, as it got halfway across the reef, it went through a ghastly series of transformations, lurching like a giant genie, changing its shape from moment to moment – a mountain, a cavern, and then some unspeakable thing, not unlike a gigantic, scaly hand ready to slap down whatever dared put itself in its path – until, after rising to an absolutely ungodly height, it inexplicably turned itself inside out and collapsed with a tremendous clap of thunder and white spray, creating a wall of bouncing white water that rushed towards them across the remainder of the shoal. Emma watched it with eyes as wide as saucers as it came closer. There was no out-running it. They didn't even try.

The wave, or its broken remnants, caught their boat like a cork toy and bounced them along on its top. For a brief moment, Emma actually thought they would ride it out. But then, it turned them sideways and one edge of their little craft dipped under the surface. The whole boat tipped up and over with an unnatural slowness and in the end, dumped the children into cold, green water.

Emma tried her best to keep her grip on the boat by digging her hands into its reed sides, but the white water wrenched it away and pushed her under too, tumbling her over in somersault after somersault. The water was cold – so cold that even though she had expected it, it still came as a shock. Her clothes felt as heavy as clay. She didn't know how deep she was, or even which way was up. The force of the wave continued to roll her head-over-heels, deeper and deeper. She cradled her arms about her skull, expecting to crash into an underwater boulder at any instant. She felt a tremendous burning in her chest, then realized it was her lungs. She had never held her breath that long before.

In truth, Emma was hardly under water more than a few seconds – eight, ten, a dozen seconds at most. It seemed much longer, but for some reason she didn't panic. Probably this is what saved her – the first time anyway – for eventually, without any effort of her own, her head popped through the surface. Emma took a deep, thankful breath.

What she had not realized, though, was that the wave had left in its trail a thick blanket of foam which coated the whole surface of the water. The foam was so light that Emma hadn't even felt it on her face when she surfaced. It was right where the air was supposed to be, and she sucked it straight into her lungs. But it was no different than breathing water. *Now* she panicked. She coughed and coughed, breathing in more of the watery foam each time. Her lungs ached with a sharpness she had never imagined. Yet there was nothing she could do. The sea began to close over her again.

The burning in her lungs was now unbearable, and the ugly, watery, gray-green surrounding her vexed her so much that she closed her eyes. So this is what it's like to drown, she thought. This is what it's like to die. But if she was dying, then it wasn't exactly the way she had always heard dying described – there was no tunnel ending in bright light, for instance, nor did she see memories from her whole life flash before her. However she did, oddly enough, imagine voices – or maybe just one voice – she thought she heard someone say, "Your hand! Give me your hand!" The voice was faraway, distant. But it repeated itself so urgently that she finally obeyed and lifted an arm, even though it caused her to sink that much faster. Just when she was sure the voice was a cruel, wishful trick that came with dying, strong fingers wrapped around her wrist, as though from a different world and, quicker than a flash, she was hauled painfully up and out of the water, over the wooden edge of a boat.

She rolled onto her back, gasping, coughing. She pushed the hair and water from her eyes, shielding them from the bright light of day. And when she could see again, she found she was staring up into the face of Rascal Pratt. He watched her for a moment until she took a breath of air. Then he hopped back to his seat, took up his oars and pulled on them smartly, first just one and then both together.

Emma pushed herself up and, to her surprise, as she tried to get her bearings on what had happened and where she was exactly, she found Sue. Sue was sitting next to her on the floor of the boat, with her head on her knees, crying. Emma stared at her for a while, not comprehending what her friend was doing, until she discovered that like Sue, she was crying too. Just then, the boat lurched again, as Rascal Pratt hopped out of his seat yet another time and leaned over the side. *Plunk*! – like magic – Harris Cole dropped into the bottom of the boat, just the other side of the center bench. And as quickly as before, Rascal Pratt was back at his oars.

The three children sitting on the floor of the dory were altogether miserable: cold, wet, and horribly shaken, and also quite uncomfortable – as it turned out, they were sharing the floor of the dory with a sharp-edged pick-axe and also a shovel, which, in spite of what they had suspected of Rascal Pratt's plans, now seemed very out of place, out here on the wet and bouncing waters of the Pacific Ocean. Each of the three rescued friends was either coughing or crying, some were doing both, and all struggling to breathe. But certainly, they were alive, and Emma, at least, was very happy to be that way. "Rascal Pratt!" she sputtered, "But how?"

"In a minute, Emma," said Rascal Pratt. "Let's get off this shoal. These are strange waters." He bent all his weight into the oars, as Emma sat there stupidly, wondering of all the things she might have wondered, if this was the first time Rascal Pratt had ever called her by her first name.

At that moment, the dory hit another wave. The little boat was now full of people and floated low in the water. Rascal Pratt changed course enough to take the wave directly on the sharp of the bow and punched gracefully through it. Then, he turned the dory north, away from the waves, and in a few strokes, scooted them out of harm's way. He paused for the briefest moment to wipe his forehead but then got straight back to work. For a long while he pulled at the oars silently and steadily, with hardly a change to his expression.

In the meantime, Sue picked herself up off the floor of the boat. She moved to the seat closest to her, which was in the bow, and sat down again, now facing rearward. As she did, she seemed to take an interest in the pick and the shovel, and touched them with her bare toe, her shoes, like those of Emma, now lost somewhere under the sea. But like Rascal Pratt, she seemed content not to speak.

Harris, meanwhile, moved to the seat in the stern. He held Achilles' double-ended paddle in his hands – Rascal Pratt had somehow fished it out of the water. Harris didn't use it though. He just held it quietly on his knees and stared down at the floor of the boat, looking very wet and utterly humiliated.

Last of all, bobbing along behind them, came Achilles' little reed boat. Miraculously, unfathomably, Rascal Pratt had rescued it as well and tied it to the back of the dory. It showed surprisingly little damage, mostly where its passengers had tried to hold onto the reeds and ended up pulling them out of their lashings. So with everyone and everything accounted for, except the girls' shoes, and with every cause for elation, it was indeed an odd silence that fell over them all – at least from Emma's point of view. But she didn't dare break it.

She shivered. Sue moved over in the seat in the bow and motioned for Emma to join her. This got Emma off the wet floor, plus Sue was warm sitting next to her. Emma half-wished Rascal Pratt would drop her off at one of the little beaches they passed every so often so she could make her own way home by land. At the same time, however, she was very curious to find out where he was going. He wore a determined look on his face which she caught a glimpse of every time he turned to look over his shoulder to see where he was going, and she wasn't quite sure she trusted him.*

They rowed on for another half hour and still no one said a word. Once, one of Rascal Pratt's passengers – or captives, whichever they were – absent-mindedly dragged a hand in the water outside the boat, making a gurgling sound that broke the silence. It was Sue, and compared to the quiet, it sounded so loud as to be positively startling, and she pulled her hand back into the boat immediately.

For Emma, this was simply too much. She, for one, thought it would be better if one of them said something, and she didn't mind being the one to do it. She decided to start with something polite.

"Thank you for rescuing us, Rascal Pratt," she tried. That seemed polite enough. "I don't think we would have made it."

Rascal Pratt nodded.

Emma had obviously hoped for more of a response than this. She thought again about what else she might say. "You

---

*One difference between the boats the Indians used (like canoes and kayaks and sakas) and rowboats, which almost everyone of European descent uses, is that in rowboats, the person rowing faces the rear of the boat and has to look over his shoulder every so often to keep himself on course. While in the sakas of the Miwok and the canoes and kayaks of other Indians, the person paddling looks quite naturally in the direction they are traveling. I believe I should prefer the native method and their paddles, though my father swears by the oars and sweeps of a rowed vessel. *(E.G.)*

saved us," she said. "You really and truly saved our lives!"

Again Rascal Pratt nodded in agreement. "You were goners, all right."

This was something at least, and Emma laughed nervously. "Well, you did say even a child could handle one of those reed boats."

"That was in the old days," grunted Rascal Pratt between strokes at the oars. "You'd a' been all right if you had stayed in the cove."

"Maybe, but you can hardly blame us. We were just trying to catch up with you."

"I didn't exactly want any company," said Rascal Pratt.

Emma sighed. Now she was tired of being polite, and she said, "You know, why don't you just put us back on shore? Wouldn't that be easier for you?"

She fully expected a sarcastic answer, something along the lines of "I think I will." But Rascal Pratt simply kept rowing and said without any hint of sarcasm, "I would, but I don't have time. Spring tide. Lowest tide of the month.*

---

*Not all high tides are the same. And not all low tides are either. You can have high highs, medium-sized highs, and low highs. And it's the same with the low tides. The heights of the highs and lows change daily and pretty much follow the moon. The lowest lows and highest highs occur when the moon is full or when the moon is new. These are called spring tides, even though they don't have anything to do with the season of spring. (The spring equinox can have an effect, but that's more complicated.) There is also something called a *neap tide* that happens when the moon is either in its first or third quarter (when you see exactly half of the moon). The neap tides aren't as extreme as the other tides during the month. They are the most moderate during the cycle. The word neap comes from the old English word "nep", but (and *I* think this is interesting anyway) no one knows what nep means, except the neap tide. That makes it an *element* of our language! (E.G.)

It's got to be today." That was the last thing he said, no matter what else Emma asked him.

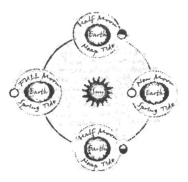

On they rowed, still moving north along the coast. They maintained a distance of about a hundred yards from shore, sometimes more, sometimes less. After a while they came to a vast stretch where sharp projections of rock jutted from the water all about. They rowed among these half-submerged boulders for another half mile, until at long last, Rascal Pratt stopped. He shipped his oars – resting them against the stern, one on either side of Harris – and announced, "Well, here we are."

Emma, along with everyone else, looked about. She had never been this far north of the lighthouse, not even on foot, and now she saw why. There were no beaches, as towering cliffs rose straight up from the ocean and were broken only by sheer ravines. And the spot Rascal Pratt had chosen to stop was completely isolated from both land and water. Any boat much larger than their dory would have had a difficult time threading its way through the rocks all around them. No, someone really would have needed a good reason to visit this place.

"Where exactly is 'here'?" asked Emma.

"*Here* is the place we start looking."

"And what are we looking for?"

"Oh, I think you know," said Rascal Pratt. "For a rock, a big, green rock. Funny color for a rock called 'The Pretty Red'. Of course, it isn't on account of its color that it got that name, now is it, Miss Green?"

"How's that?" said Emma. She didn't quite catch Rascal Pratt's drift.

"You don't have to pretend," said Rascal Pratt. "I heard you talking with your father last night."

"Last night?"

"Sure, while you were eating supper."

"My goodness, were you spying on us?" Emma burst out indignantly. In truth, she knew she was overreacting at least a little – but *still*! "Were you spying on us while we were having our supper?"

"Spying?" Rascal Pratt repeated with a sly wink. "Now, is *that* what you call it? I suppose you would know – it *is* such common practice in these parts – listening in on other folks' conversations. Or following them wherever they go."

Emma reddened and started to protest, but Rascal Pratt waved her off. "Oh, don't worry, it really doesn't matter. It's just that when I heard you talking to your father about the Pretty Red, I knew I had to act fast. If I let the spring tide go by, I'd have to wait another couple of weeks. Treasure doesn't stay hidden long once the word is out."

"But you can't be serious," said Emma. "You can't really be looking for treasure – and certainly not Sir Francis Drake's. The age of piracy was a hundred and fifty years ago, and Drake landed here a hundred and fifty years before that – if he landed here at all."

"I never said it was Sir Francis Drake," said Rascal Pratt, "though I admit, it's hard to guess who else's treasure it could be. But some sort of talk came down through the years to Achilles. He's not one to make up a thing like that – or to get it wrong. He asked me to do this for him. So, I'm doing it." Rascal Pratt looked at the others in the boat, and then glanced uncomfortably away.

It was quiet in the boat for a bit. They each peered out over the waters around them, as though trying to guess whether the old legend could possibly contain any truth. A V-shaped formation of pelicans glided silently by, and nearly all eyes turned to watch it.

At length, Sue spoke. "Rascal Pratt," she said quietly, "I don't doubt you're looking for treasure. But don't blame Emma and Harris. I'm the one who wanted to follow you. I know Achilles trusts you. But he's my grandfather, and he's old. So I have to ask: let's say you do find treasure – what's to stop you from keeping it, all of it? I don't mean to offend you, I just... I have to know."

A pained look crossed Rascal Pratt's face. He was silent for some time, then sighed and said, "Fair enough. I won't take offense – I know you're thinking of your grandfather. But I still don't have a good answer for you. I only know that I intend to keep my word – maybe just because Achilles does trust me. I don't know why, but he trusted me from the very beginning, you see, and not many people do."

"And I don't mean to distrust you, Rascal Pratt," said Sue quickly. "It's just that so many things don't make sense. Why now, for instance? If Achilles has known for all these years that there was treasure out here, how come he never came to look for it?"

Rascal Pratt shrugged. "Maybe he didn't care about treasure before. Not everyone does, you know. Some people think treasure is cursed, especially if it was stolen from someone else to begin with – and most treasure was. Achilles is the only person I ever met who'd be happy growing older and older without any sort of treasure at all. But things change I guess, and curses wear off. As luck would have it, a certain need has presented itself just when Achilles' eyesight is nearly gone and he's too old to search for treasure himself."

"A need?" Sue echoed. "What need, may I ask?"

Rascal Pratt shifted in his seat without answering.

"Well, what need is it?" Sue repeated. "You're the one who said it. You must know what it is."

"But you know this already," Rascal Pratt protested softly. "And if you don't, it isn't for me to tell."

"I know already? But I don't. I don't know at all!"

"Well, you must know at least that everything changed when you came to live with him."

Sue laughed. "I'm sure things did change for the poor old man, used as he was to living by himself! But I'm not so spoiled that I need a treasure to be happy. It's true, I do say silly things sometimes, like I'm going to Europe to study opera and ballet. But that's just talk, and everyone knows it. It can't be that." She looked suspiciously at Rascal Pratt. "Or is it? If you know, I want you to tell me!"

The ocean was flat all around them, aside from an occasional rise and fall as a low swell rolled underneath them. They were several hundred yards from shore. Not a living soul was in sight, only the seals that basked on rocks jutting here and there above the surface.

Rascal Pratt exhaled and leaned over to pick out of the floorboards a stray nub of wood left over from the repair of his boat. He tossed it over the side and glanced uncomfortably over his shoulder, especially at Harris, and then to Sue he said, "No, it's not to get you to Europe. It's only to get you to San Francisco. It's to buy your freedom, of course. Achilles' freedom, and yours."

For such simple words, these last made no sense – not to Emma anyway, who quite naturally had been following the conversation between Sue and Rascal Pratt closely. The words fell like bombs and burst audibly in gasps of disbelief about the boat. Emma looked back and forth between the two, between Sue and Rascal Pratt, with no idea what they were talking about.

Harris, however, cried out, "What in the world are you saying? Sue is as free as any of us!"

Rascal Pratt seemed uninterested in an argument. And with great fatigue he said, "Is she, Harris? Achilles has not been free one day his whole life. And now that Sue has come to live with him, no one knows if she is either. Her own parents were free, true enough, but now they're dead. Sue Hermanastra is now simply Sue, an Indian, granddaughter of a slave."

"What slave?" cried Harris. "Why, you're mad – you're completely cracked! I don't know how things are where you're from, but this is the United States, and Achilles is free, just like the rest of us. Yeah, he's our right-hand man on the rancho and we'd never *want* him to leave. He's practically family – but he *is* free to leave if he wants, and Sue is too."

Rascal Pratt shrugged. "Suit yourself," he said quietly.

"Do you know what you are, Rascal Pratt?" Harris went on hotly. "You're just a little... a little *troublemaker*!"

At that moment, Rascal Pratt happened to be facing the two girls in the bow. Emma saw his eyes flash, and he spun around and said through gritted teeth, "You know, I'm tired of being called names by you, Mr. Cole, and this is the last time I'm going to let it go. If you don't believe what I'm saying is true, then get up some guts and ask your father. Ask him what would happen if Achilles quit and took Sue to live in San Francisco. Ask him! Achilles is bound to the land. How could you have lived with him so long and never known? Do you just not care? He was part of the rancho before it ever came into your family, and by an old agreement, he can't leave until he pays off an ancient debt. No one even remembers what the debt is. If Achilles tries to leave, he'll end up in jail. Say what you want, but it *is* true."

"No, it's not!" cried Harris. "It isn't!" He was white with anger, and he stood in the stern of the boat, pointing his finger at Rascal Pratt, shaking as he shouted, "You're a liar! Sue, he's a liar. Don't believe him, don't believe a word he says!"

The boat lurched under Harris's outburst, and Sue grabbed her bench to steady herself. "Harris, Harris, sit down!" she said before anyone else had a chance to react. "You'll turn the whole boat over." She looked away and sighed. Then she looked back to her childhood friend, her almost-brother, and said gently, "What Rascal Pratt is saying about Achilles is true, Harris. I've known for some time. My mother told me just before she died."

Harris stared at Sue in an awful combination of stupefaction and betrayal. "But why," he finally stammered, "why did you not tell me?"

Sue moved awkwardly on the little bench in the bow and looked down at the floor of the boat. "I... I don't know, Harris. Honestly, I guess I just thought it could never change. I know you love him too. I... I'm sorry."

"But you should have," moaned Harris, who was plainly and deeply hurt, "maybe we could have done something sooner. You should have said *something*."

"I know, Harris, I know. And I'm sorry I didn't. But what if... you couldn't change it? Or what if your father wouldn't? Then would we have hated each other? I'm not sure if I could stand that. Harris, listen, I know this is coming all at once, and that makes it especially hard. But think about it, this is actually *good* news, what Rascal Pratt is saying – treasure or not, it sounds like Achilles thinks that maybe there *is* a way out. If anyone knows, it's Achilles."

Harris only stared at her. At last his mouth, with great effort, twisted open, but no words came out. He seemed to be trying to say too many things at once. So many expressions crossed his brow, one after the other: expressions of pain, disbelief, and also something else, something akin to shame, but a profound and unbearable one. Uncertainly, he put his hands down behind him and lowered himself to his seat.

Now it really was quiet, much more so than before. The silence was almost too heavy for the little boat, and Emma felt she should not have been there at all. Someone had to say something. But a long while passed before anyone did. It was Sue who broke it in the end – after all, who else could it have been? She tossed another nub of wood into the water, another little scrap left over from the repair of the dory, and as they all watched, the rings grew from the place it landed until they encircled the boat and separated the four of them from the whole vastness of the sea.

"Well, what are we waiting for?" she said, suddenly stirring. "If Achilles sent us out here, let's get to work! Tell us again, Rascal Pratt, what did you say we're looking for?"

- 9 -
The Pretty Red

All around them, the sun danced off the water. Unearthly formations of stone broke the surface here and there. Some jutted up sharply, and others were broad and low and covered with sleeping seals who woke from time to time, especially the little ones, and blinked curiously through their round, dark eyes at the four passengers of the dory. A lazy breeze barely moved the air. To Emma it was mostly unnoticeable, and she was scarcely more aware of the movements of the sea, which heaved dreamily and occasionally under their keel, like the breast of an enormous, napping beast.

"It's an unusual rock," said Rascal Pratt, "that's how Achilles said we'd know it."

"But there are thousands of rocks here," said Sue. "And they're all strange, if you ask me. What makes this one so unusual?"

"Well, as I said, it's not actually red, it's green.* And according to Achilles, it's due west of a V made from two tall hills." Rascal Pratt pointed towards the shore. Two steep hills came together to form a valley and the line where they joined made a V-shaped notch in the green of the cliffs. It was the only place as far as Emma could see where the blue of the sky came down through the hills all the way to the water. "So there's the V. Which means that out here somewhere is the rock." He waved his arm in a broad circle around them. "It's also the largest rock in a group of three. And Achilles says the real sign is that the rock has a window in it – a big arch, big enough to paddle a boat through. The floor of the arch is usually underwater, though at low tides, it's just a couple of feet deep. Achilles was very sure about this. So I was thinking: maybe the treasure is buried under the arch. That way you

---

*The coast here is very rocky and I find all kinds of rocks that I don't know much about. But there are two in particular that seem to make up a lot of the cliffs and such, and my mother has helped me find out about them. One is sort of rust red, the other is gray-green. The red one is called "Chert," and it looks like a lot of little layers that are sometimes turned on their end. I've heard it's fossilized clay and planktons. Planktons are, of course, little living things in the water. A lot of the cliffs seem to be made of it. And the green one is called "Green Serpentine." I've even heard it referred to as jade, though it isn't really, at least not the one here. It's an igneous rock – old volcanic rock – and it came from deep under the earth's surface many millions of years ago. *(E.G.)*

could find it again only on the lowest tides, and even then you'd have to search underwater."

"Wait," interrupted Sue, "you think they buried the treasure underwater?"

"Well, why not?" said Rascal Pratt. "It's very clever if you ask me. Unless someone landed on the rock on just the right day, on a low, spring tide for instance, they wouldn't ever find the place, not even by accident. And even if they did come on a very low tide, they'd still have to go to the extra trouble of searching under a few feet of water."

As Rascal Pratt and Sue continued to debate the likelihood of Rascal Pratt's theory, Emma looked around her. And indeed, just off to her left, not twenty yards away, was a formation composed of three rocks. "Oh, look, three rocks!" she cried. But then a moment later she added, "Wait, there's another bunch of three. And another." But even with her enthusiasm somewhat blunted, she still continued to point out various rock formations, particularly if one had some peculiar feature to recommend it. Sue joined her. But each time they called another to his attention, Rascal Pratt found some shortcoming.

"Not green enough," he said. "Not big enough." Or, "No arch." Also, it was difficult to know when they really were due west of the cleft in the hills. Rascal Pratt kept saying he could tell from the angle of the sun, but every few minutes, he picked up the oars and rowed a few dozen strokes to yet another spot, each time announcing that now they were *exactly* due west of the V-shaped notch. And meanwhile, Harris said nothing. He only sat silently, looking at the floor of the boat.

Rascal Pratt let the boat drift with the oars still in their locks. He rested his elbows on his knees and put his head

in his hands while he rubbed his eyes. He didn't touch the oars again for some time. Suddenly, though, it occurred to Emma that the dory, which all day seemed to have had the current behind it, now no longer moved in any direction. It remained perfectly still. Rascal Pratt must have noticed it too, for he lifted his head from his hands and exclaimed, "Slack water – the tide will be turning soon. We don't have much time."

And so, they all began to look with renewed energy. Even Harris joined in and made a suggestion or two about this group of rocks or that. But, among the hundreds of rocks, there just wasn't one that seemed to fit the description.

By then, the time was well beyond noon. A band of silver shimmered on the horizon, and a little puff of air moved across the water, the first breath of the afternoon sea breeze. As far as breezes went, it was still quite light, especially for those parts. Over time, though, the breeze pushed the dory off the line Rascal Pratt had been holding and nudged them closer to a strange formation of four large rocks that they had been using as a reference point.

Two rocks of the four were enormous stone pillars, each ten yards or so in diameter. Both these columns were green, while from the water next to each jutted a much smaller rock, like a knee, each knee reddish in color, though capped like everything else out there with the white and gray of bird droppings.

It was about then that Emma heard a scraping sound.

"Drat it," muttered Rascal Pratt, "we're aground." He lifted an oar out of the locks and started to pole the boat off the reef underneath them with the handle of the oar shaft. But then he stopped and said again, "Wait – we're *aground!*"

"Isn't that a bad thing?" asked Emma.

"Normally it's bad," said Rascal Pratt, "if you care about the bottom of your boat. But now..." He didn't finish his thought. He simply stood there squinting up at each of the green pillars, shading his eyes with his hand. The two pillars towered over the boat. Rascal Pratt scratched his chin and said softly, "Could *this* be it?"

"But it's not an arch," said Sue, "and it's four rocks, not three."

"Yes," said Rascal Pratt, excitedly now, pointing to the curve in both pillars, "but imagine an arch from this rock to that one. See how they curve towards each other? Maybe it was three rocks instead of four, so many years ago, when Achilles heard the tale – or three hundred years ago, when they hid the treasure. Don't you see? The arch has collapsed – that's what we ran into. The arch fell and covered the old floor! And now there are four rocks instead of three."

They all leaned over to the left side of the boat to get a better look. The dory teetered underneath them. "Careful, everyone," cautioned Rascal Pratt. "We're gonna get wet soon enough. If this is where the treasure's buried, we've got our work cut out for us. There must be a couple of tons of stone right on top of the place we are supposed to be looking – and all of it under a couple of feet of water."

He maneuvered the dory over to one of the columns. He anchored out the stern and tied the bow to the rock itself, then he climbed from the dory onto the rock. One by one, the other three joined him. If nothing else, Emma was glad to have something solid under her at last and to stretch her legs. Harris came over last with the pick-axe and the shovel.

"Well," said Emma, "where do we start?"

"I don't know," said Rascal Pratt as he stepped from rock

to rock like a little goat, though he favored his good leg, "But the tide's coming in now and we don't have much time to figure it out."

Just then Emma heard a *ka-sploosh,* and then another, and looking behind her, she saw Harris lift a piece of rubble from the shallow water that stretched between the two columns and throw it into the deeper water off to the side. He mopped his brow.

"Well, that's the hard way," he said. "We couldn't move all this rock if we had a hundred full-moon tides. We must be missing something." He turned to Rascal Pratt and started to ask, "If *you* buried—," but he stopped himself, and for a while it seemed he was wrestling with something no one else could see. Finally, he swallowed and started again, saying "If *you* buried the treasure, Rascal Pratt, where would you have put it?"

The two boys stared at one another for a long while, neither moving. At length, Rascal Pratt nodded and answered, "I don't rightly know, Harris. In a place like this, I suppose I'd try to find a crack deep in the rock and then fit some stones on top of it. You can't really dig here with a shovel."

There was another long length of silence, and then Harris nodded too. "Well, all right then," he said, "let's look for a crack." And then to everyone he added "But here's the thing – if they buried whatever it is we're looking for in the old floor of the arch, it's got to be underwater now. The water's pretty clear here. It looks like we might do best swimming in the deeper water along side of the old floor and looking that way. Looking from the side's the only way – with all this rock that fell from the roof, we'll never get to it from the top."

Rascal Pratt and Sue nodded, but Emma said with alarm, "You don't mean swim – under the water – do you?"

"Sure," said Harris, "it's not so hard you know, and the water is pretty clear."

"But..." protested Emma. Her last encounter with the water was enough to last her for a long time and she didn't think Harris and Sue had proven themselves to be such fabulous swimmers either.

"Harris is right," said Rascal Pratt. "And I'll do it. After all, Achilles is giving me a share. I should at least do a little bit of work—"

"No," said Harris suddenly. He said it surprisingly loudly, and when they all turned to look at him, he added quietly, "I just mean, I want to. I'd like to help – if I can."

"Oh, Harris, you already are," said Sue. "We all are."

"All the same, I'd like to do this. Now, Rascal Pratt, don't you have a rope or something I can hold onto?"

Rascal Pratt studied Harris one more time, and then he nodded, "Sure, here's a line. I'll loop it around your waist – but you should hold onto it too, right here."

Harris took the rope and started to untie his shoes.

"Leave your shoes on," said Sue. "The rock is sharp and there are lots of barnacles."

Harris stopped untying his shoes and laced them back.

"And don't get too close to the rock," said Rascal Pratt, "You don't want to knock your head."

Harris peered into the water and nodded.

"And— " Emma began to say.

"Enough already!" cried Harris, "would everyone let me do this?"

"I - I only wanted to say, be careful, Harris," said Emma bashfully.

Harris smiled at her and promised he would. Then he set about lowering himself into the water.

He climbed over the edge until he was standing on a boulder a few feet below the surface. Sue held onto the rope. Harris pulled several lengths of slack through her hands, then took a deep breath and blew his cheeks out like a chipmunk. He ducked under water and began feeling about the rock. A wave hit the front of the Pretty Red just then. Little eddies of moving water swirled around back to where Harris was and made it hard for him to stay in one place. But he continued working along the shelf for a few more yards before coming up for air.

"Anything?" shouted Rascal Pratt when Harris surfaced.

Harris shook his head, took another breath, and went under again. And again he came up for air. He took another breath and sank back down into the water. But after three or four breaths like this, as he was making his way farther along the jumble of boulders that stretched between the two green pillars, a much larger wave approached the front of the Pretty Red. As it did, it sucked water away from the back of the formation, drawing it over the sharp rocks of the submerged floor of the arch. With the water, went Harris.

It happened so quickly that by the time Harris hit the end of the safety line they had rigged for him, he was moving quite fast. Sue was unprepared for the shock of it and the rope went spinning through her hands before she had a chance to realize what was happening. Harris came up to the surface immediately, his eyes wide with fear. He had been dragged across the rock shelf and out to sea, cut off from the view of the others, who were gathered on the landward side of the formation of rock.

"Harris!" Emma screamed.

Rascal Pratt hobbled on his bad leg over the pile of rubble to the ocean side of the rock as another wave hit. Emma felt something sliding underfoot just then and realized that she was stepping on Harris's line. She stamped hard on it. It went taut but it pulled so hard that she knew Harris must still be attached to it, and she reached down quickly and began to pull it in. The current had reversed itself as water from the next wave started to flow back across the submerged floor of rock to the landward side. And looking out to the very place where she had seen Harris disappear, Emma saw him reappear, now pushed by the wave. He was clutching his line for dear life and struggling to keep his head above water.

Emma, Sue, and Rascal Pratt – all three reeled madly in on Harris's lifeline. With the help of the second wave, which pushed Harris back toward them, he was soon at their feet once again.

"Harris, Harris, are you all right?" asked Emma frantically, as they helped Harris out of the water. "You gave me such a fright!" Sue in the meantime was busy inspecting Harris's back. It was covered with scrapes and red welts.

"Don't worry about me," said Harris, shaking them all off, "I'm fine, I'm fine," and actually he did seem very excited about something. "But listen, we're looking in the wrong spot!"

"What do you mean?" said Rascal Pratt.

"Well, come see for yourself!"

So Harris led them around the base of the rock, toward the sea. On the far side, not quite facing the ocean, a sharp little finger of rock jutted straight up. It protected a small crevice, not only from the brunt of the ocean, but also from sight. If you were at just the right angle, however, you could see into the crevice and make out something odd at its very end. At first, it was hard to see, but when Emma looked carefully she saw that one side of the crevice was not of natural rock. It was a wall of a different sort of stone. And clearly, it was built by human hands.

"Ballast!" exclaimed Rascal Pratt.

"I beg your pardon?" said Emma.

"Yes, *ballast,* that's what those stones are. Long ago, they used stones like that as ballast in ships. It's weight, it keeps the keel down and the decks up. Anyway, see how they're all the same size?"

The four of them made their way cautiously into the crevice. It was narrow and probably would only have fit one adult. But they all wedged themselves in anyway and crowded right up to the wall. The ballast stones were tightly laid, but probing here and there, they found one they could wiggle in its place. This caused great excitement to run through them all, so great that no one thought to go get the tools they had left on the other side of the rock. They all took turns digging at the one, loose stone with bare hands and fingernails, and at long last, they succeeded in wiggling it all the way out of its place, though they cut and bruised their hands and fingers in the process. It was clear by then that there was a small cave behind the wall, which had been sealed for who knew how long. It wasn't pleasant work, as a terrible odor drifted out through the hole they had made.

"Phew!" exclaimed Harris with a look of repugnance. "So that's what three hundred years smells like. If ever a living thing gets trapped in there, probably it never gets out. Rank!"

The four of them kept working though, and soon enough they had cleared enough of the ballast stones to peer inside. It was dark in the cave, and it took Emma's eyes a full minute to adjust to it. But when she did, her heart sank. She saw that the cave was empty, obviously empty.

Beside her, however, and to Emma's great puzzlement, Rascal Pratt was having the exact opposite reaction. He frantically began to claw away the rest of the stones that blocked the opening and throw them behind him, stone after stone, not caring who was at his back. Cries of "Careful!" came from his three friends as they did their best to get out of the shower of heavy stones, "Stop!"

At last Rascal Pratt did stop. He had succeeded in opening a passage large enough for a child to crawl through. Now, however, the smell issuing from inside the rock was simply outrageous. Emma could safely say she had never smelled anything that bad before. It was the smell of rotting fish, rotting seaweed, rotting barnacles, maybe even rotting baby seals. It was the smell of the sea. Emma clutched her stomach. Without any hesitation though, Rascal Pratt took a breath and on all fours crawled through the opening. Emma glanced at Sue and Harris with a nauseous expression on her face. But Sue peered into the opening, took a deep breath of fresh air, and she too disappeared through the passage they had made. After her, Harris did the same.

Emma was now alone on the outside of the cave, on the ledge, on the rock, surrounded by a sparkling expanse of blue-black water. The sky spread over her, an arch of its own, from silver and blue at the horizon to something almost purple at its highest point, directly overhead. A light breeze was fresh in her face, and it too smelled of the sea – the good sea, the living sea. Slowly though, she turned back to the place her friends had disappeared. Her eyes were once again accustomed to daylight, and in the rock, the cave was only an oily, black hole. And the smell, oh, the smell! It brought her stomach into her throat again, but she set her teeth together, swallowed hard, and thought, *I am going in there too.*

And then, she was in. She gagged, then panted at the floor for a few seconds, long enough for her eyes to adjust to the dark. She lifted her head and, through the gloom, she saw her friends on hands and knees, gathered over what appeared to be a fissure – a sort of ditch that ran through the rough rock floor. Rascal Pratt was already busy removing stones from it – and not just stones, Emma saw, but square, perfectly hewn bricks. On all fours, Emma crawled to join them.

By now the tide had risen high enough that a surge from a wave caused a small stream of water to trickle across the cave floor into the fissure where Rascal Pratt was working. He worked faster. Suddenly he stopped. There, wedged into the crack was a small chest. It looked exactly the sort of thing you saw in books about pirates: a funny, round top and a rusted lump of something that must have once been a lock.

Rascal Pratt stepped over the fissure to the far side. "Emma," he said, since it was Emma who was now exactly opposite him, "See that handle there? Grab it, would you? On three, let's lift – it might be heavy."

Rascal Pratt counted 'three.' They both pulled. Emma pulled with all she was worth. The chest didn't budge. Again, Rascal Pratt counted three. This time all of the company pulled, by whatever they could get hold of. Again the chest didn't budge. They kept pulling, straining, and grunting. Then, there was a loud *crack!* They all tumbled backwards onto the floor, with bits of wood and leather in their hands. And when they got up, they saw that the chest had fallen apart under the strain of its own weight. Its pieces were floating in the water that filled the bottom of the crevice. Emma, and everyone else, gasped. For in the fissure, under a few inches of water, lay what looked like thousands of coins the color of the sun. Not a brassy, tawdry yellow, but a soft yellow, a beautiful yellow, softer than the color of straw, yet somehow luminescent, even in the gloom of the cave.

Very slowly, Rascal Pratt reached out and took one of the coins in his hand. He held it to the little bit of light that came through the cave door. "A doubloon," he said in a whisper. "A real... Spanish... doubloon."

"How much is it worth?" asked Emma breathlessly, and for some reason whispering too. "Is it enough to..."

"Well, I'd say these coins must each weigh an ounce – an ounce of gold." Rascal Pratt handed the piece to Sue. "I reckon you've got enough gold here to pay off the debt – and buy a house in San Francisco, too."

Sue held the gold piece in her fingers. Emma tried to imagine what it meant to her. Just an hour ago Sue had spoken of her own grandfather as a man who was essentially a slave, who had never in his whole life been free to go where he pleased. Now she had enough gold to take him wherever he wanted. Where would he want to go, Emma wondered. Where would Sue want to go?

For Emma, up until that moment, the chief beauty of the yellow river that ran through the gloom of the cave was simply the adventure of it – how the four of them, as friends, had found it. But now it occurred to her that almost certainly, everything would change. Sue and Achilles would not stay at Point Bonita, for who would stay, free or otherwise, with this much gold at their fingertips?

The Mystery of Rascal Pratt

- 10 -
No Entry

Rascal Pratt rowed and rowed. The ocean rolled gently and the breeze freshened somewhat, though it remained light and swung to the north. The little dory, originally built for two passengers, now rode very low in the water indeed, carrying the four of them, and enough gold coin to cover the whole floor of the boat. Even with the wind behind them, it would be a slow journey home.

That day, many new things had happened. Even so, it was a strange thing for Emma to see so much gold just lying in the bottom of the dory, and, on top it, their anchor, their shovel, even their feet. Lacking sacks or buckets or anything else, they had carried the gold coins out of the cave in their bare hands, for almost an hour, handful after handful, back to the dory. The water in the cave rose a little deeper with each trip, as they raced against the rising tide. But in the end, they took it all, every coin they could find.

By late afternoon, they finally drew even with a broad, sand beach. Emma recognized it – it was called Rodeo Beach, the beach just over the hill from her house. She seldom visited it, since, unlike today, it was usually cold, blustery, and deserted, as it faced northwest and therefore the relentless wind off the sea. But today it was warm and comparatively calm, and Emma noticed that a man was standing on the shore. The man was tall and thin, and leaned on a staff. Even at that distance, it was impossible not to recognize Achilles.

Rascal Pratt angled the dory toward the beach, rowing closer and closer, until he was just outside the breaking waves. He waited until a wave passed underneath the keel of the laden little boat, then rowed hard just behind it, so as not to get caught on its face and have his boat turned over. He followed the wave all the way to the beach, until the dory's bottom scraped heavily against the sand.

Achilles waited for them, standing in ankle deep water now, and with a quickness that took Emma by surprise, he found their boat as though by sound alone and pulled it up onto dry sand before the next wave came up behind them. Rascal Pratt hopped out beside him. The line to the reed boat they had towed behind the dory was already in his hand. He pulled it lightly up onto the beach beside the dory.

"I understand you found company," said Achilles, nodding to Emma, Harris, and Sue, though they had not yet spoken a word.

"Yes, I did," said Rascal Pratt, "and it's a good thing too." He leaned into the boat and rattled his hands through the coins. Then he picked one up and put it in Achilles' palm.

For a long while, Achilles stood utterly motionless, as still as the ageless stones, not even closing his fingers over the thing Rascal Pratt had placed in his palm. At long last, after more than one wave had washed over his feet, did he allow himself any movement, and handing the piece to Sue, he said, "Tell me what it looks like, granddaughter. Is there a likeness of a mountain?"

Sue took the piece from him and looked at it closely. "No, Grandfather, there is not."

"Is there a sun?"

"No, Grandfather, there is not."

Achilles sighed with a sad smile. "It's not important. Something I once read in a book. For many years I have imagined it that way." Then his smiled brightened and he said, "So then, tell me, my dear, what *does* it look like? From what little I can see, it's yellow at least."

"Oh, yes," said Sue. "Wonderfully so." She went on to describe the piece. She told him all the things she saw on it – a cross, some curious-looking designs she didn't understand, and some numbers. Achilles stood all the while with his hands on the rails of Rascal Pratt's dory. He might have been looking at the pile of gold, except his eyes were closed. Then, he shook his head and said, "So, the old stories were true. It's been there all this time. Perhaps I should not have waited so long."

117

"Better late than never, I say," said Rascal Pratt cheerfully. "You're a free man now."

Achilles smiled. "Am I? We'll soon see, I suppose. And you, my young friend? What will you do? Buy your boat and sail to Australia? Or was that just talk? Half is yours, as you know – I intend to keep my end of the bargain."

"Oh, no," said Rascal Pratt. "Maybe a handful or two, if you insist. But I don't think I could safely get back to San Francisco with much more than that. The coins are heavy, you'll find."

Achilles laughed. "We'll each find a way, I'm sure. Half is yours. That was the agreement, though for now I suppose we should just try to get it off the beach."

He had brought his cart and donkey with him, as it turned out, and also a pile of burlap sacks. With the help of Rascal Pratt and the other three youths, he began to remove exactly half of the gold from the boat, but only half, and on this, he very much insisted.

Emma made a trip to the donkey cart, and as she turned back to the beach, she happened to take notice of the sun. It was low in the sky, and for the first time in a long while, she remembered she was supposed to be on watch, back at the lighthouse.

"Oh my," she said to the others, "I have to go! If you don't mind, I think I'll just run over the hill. Rascal Pratt, finish here if you need to, it will probably be easier to row back without me anyway." And more to herself than anyone else, she added, "I wish I hadn't lost my shoes. That is what my mother will care about most!"

She said goodbye to her friends and hurried off. The walk wasn't too far, not quite a mile. Much of it was across the deep sand of the beach. The hill was steep though, and it took

Emma a while to find the way. Thick brush had overgrown at least one part of the trail. When she finally arrived at the top, she was panting, and her feet and her legs, all the way up to the hem of her cotton frock, were more than just a little scratched, and now she too was quite vexed on account of her missing shoes.

She made a wide circle around her house and walked quietly down the path to the tunnel, taking care not to overturn so much as a pebble. She tiptoed across the wooden planks of the bridge and noiselessly opened the door to the lighthouse. It was completely still inside. She climbed the ladder to the lantern room. The log lay open on the desk. And there was not a one entry for the day – it was probably the only day in the whole book for which a single vessel had not been recorded. She wondered what her father would think, and she prayed that a ship of some sort might come in before sunset so she could at least write something down.

Her eyes had not yet adjusted to the dimness inside. As she looked around trying to decide what she should do first to keep up the appearance of diligence and duty – polish the globes or wind the weights or trim the wicks – she smelled something familiar. She couldn't immediately place it. For a second she even wondered if her father was using the new kerosene fuel she had heard about. She did, just then, hear a noise behind her. But thinking it the wind, and having decided to start the evening's work by winding the weights, she didn't pay the sound any further attention. A moment later, it occurred to her what the smell was – why it was *turpentine* of all things, as if someone had been painting. Emma spun quickly around. A shadowy figure stood at the top of the ladder and Emma started with surprise, just as a voice said, "Why, hello, Emma."

Emma let out a muffled gasp and her heart nearly stopped beating. She realized then – of course – it was her mother.

"Mama!" she cried and she threw herself against her, half angry, half relieved. "*Don't* sneak up on me like that!"

"Well, if you were really on watch, perhaps I wouldn't have startled you," laughed Mabel Green. "That's why they call it *the watch*, dear – when you're really *watching*, things can't sneak up." She crossed her arms sternly in front of her and asked, "Now, do you want to tell me where you've been?"

Emma opened her mouth to answer – only she didn't know how much to say. She looked down at her dress and was glad at least it had dried. She tried to hide her bare feet by inching behind the chair. She certainly didn't want to tell her mother about nearly drowning out in the Potato Patch – that would frighten her too much. And certainly not about the treasure either. Nor yet about Achilles and Sue and the rancho, which was obviously their own private business, and theirs alone. She didn't want to lie, but what was left to tell?

"Well, Rascal Pratt, you see, took us for a boat ride," she began. "And... I'm sorry I'm late, Mother, really I am, but... you know, I don't know what it is about boats – the simplest trip can take a whole day!" Emma secretly congratulated herself for saying this, as she thought she was being very clever – she had heard her mother voice this exact complaint about boats herself, only with regard to Emma's father, Captain Green, whenever he took to the sea for pleasure.

"Yes, I saw you, you know," Mrs. Green responded sharply.

Emma's heart skipped a beat and she searched her mother's face for some sign of how much she had actually seen.

"Yes, I did," her mother went on, "I came down here

with my easel and paints, thinking to keep you company. Only when I got here, I found the lighthouse empty! I was alarmed, Emma, really I was, when I didn't find you. What did you think I would do? Luckily I looked out the window and saw you and Sue and Harris in Rascal Pratt's little boat, taking your excursion. I happened to run into Achilles who came down looking for Sue. When I told him I had just seen her with you and Harris in the boat, he said he thought you were going over to Rodeo Beach – otherwise I would have been frantic. Now, Emma, tell me the truth, isn't that boat of Rascal Pratt's too small for all of you?"

Emma looked down sheepishly. "Yes," she said, "it is."

Her mother sighed, but then she started to smile in a forgiving way. At this, Emma was actually beginning to think she had escaped somewhat easily, when suddenly Mrs. Green, who was after all a mother, exclaimed, "Emma Green? Where are your shoes?"

"My shoes?" repeated Emma.

"Yes, your shoes. Where are they?"

Emma fidgeted. "They... they fell out of the boat – it kind of tipped over. Just a little, I mean."

"Tipped over?" her mother cried. "Oh Emma, you see? This is why we worry. Now, I'm sure Rascal Pratt's an able seafarer, but what if the boat had tipped all the way over? What if you had fallen into the water? You can't even swim, you know."

"You're right, Mama," said Emma, who was now trying her absolute best to sound sorry. "You are absolutely right, and I should learn how to swim. I most strongly agree."

"Emma," sighed Mrs. Green after few seconds, "You know, I think it's all right for your father and me out here. He has his work and I have my painting. But for you, perhaps it's not fair – or healthful."

Emma suddenly had a very strange inkling that something was in the works she didn't yet know about, and she said quickly, "Oh, no, Mama, it is fair – it's very fair. *And* healthful. I like it here. And I have friends."

"Yes, I know, two friends. And Mr. Pratt too, of course, though it's just a matter of time before he leaves us. Well, I'm glad that you have them at least, really I am. But I mean real friends you can see every day. Anyway, your father and I have talked about it. We think perhaps you should go live in Sausalito."

"Sausalito?" cried Emma. "You mean, move? Me? Oh, Mama, but I *do* like it here. Why, I love it!"

"I'm sure you do, Emma. I've come to love it myself. But you should be in school. Meeting lots of people your own age, not just one or two. We'll talk about it further when your father returns. That's one reason he isn't here right now, you know. He had business in San Francisco to be sure, but he's also stopping on his way back to look at the school in Sausalito. I hadn't told you, but it seems the school needs a teacher. They've written me to see if I want the position. It might be a good thing, Emma. And it's only five miles away."

"Oh, Mother, it's seven miles, and that's if you take the foot path."

"All right, seven then. But we'd come back out here, to the Point, every few days of course, to see your father. It would be no different than when he was in the Navy. In fact, it probably would be much better, in that sense."

"Mama, I *don't* want to move," said Emma resolutely.

But Mrs. Green didn't seem to hear her anymore, and only kept repeating, "I know dear, but let's just see what your father has found out."

- 11 -
Branded

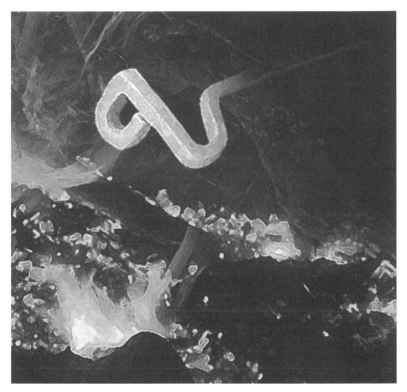

12th of May, 1866: 1 three-master, the "Pampona" from Italy; the steel hull clipper, "Luftfresser" of Prussia; 3 fishing vessels of Monterey.

The following day, right after breakfast, Mabel Green went out to the stable to hitch the mule to the wagon. Emma remained in the house, packing a meal for the journey, as the trip to meet Captain Green was bound to take all day. Emma hated the thought of taking the mule-drawn wagon. They would have to drive it along the footpath, for which it was much too wide, and she would have to hop down from the seat every few minutes to help push a wheel over a rock. It was a good thing they were getting an early start.

She was only partly done packing their food, when Rascal Pratt came downstairs. He walked into the kitchen with an obvious limp, but he had only one crutch with him, and even that one, he carried in his hand. When Emma saw him, she said, "Well now, you're awfully brave, Rascal Pratt, walking about without your aids!"

Rascal Pratt blushed, "A bit sore from all the excitement yesterday, but a little stronger every day, thanks mainly to your mother."

"She'll be happy to hear that, I'm sure," said Emma, "only, you still have a *prodigious* limp and you'll hurt yourself again if you aren't careful. Anyway, it's no secret you've been walking without your crutches for a few days now. What's so different about today that you no longer hide it?"

Rascal Pratt didn't answer and when Emma glanced up from her work, he looked quickly away.

"What is it?" said Emma raising an eyebrow. "Something really is different about today, isn't it?"

Rascal Pratt turned to face her. He wore an awkward expression, and he said, "Well, to tell you the truth, I suppose something is different. It's... it's time for me to be going – I'll be leaving soon, I mean. I guess that's what makes today different."

Emma however only laughed, and she said, "What you really mean is, you're rich now, and you don't need us anymore!"

"Not exactly," said Rascal Pratt, "but a little gold in the pocket does make certain practical points of leaving easier."

"Ah, I see," said Emma, teasingly. "So are you going to buy a boat then, like Achilles said? A fine sailing ship, and sail out of San Francisco? If it's a pirate ship, could you raise the Jolly Roger and fire a cannon on your way out the Golden Gate? It would be grand to hear the boom!"

"That's very funny," said Rascal Pratt. "But just you watch, that's what I'll do."

"You know, you can stop pretending – I know you're not a pirate." Emma was still speaking lightheartedly, yet when she said this, a shadow passed over Rascal Pratt's face, and so she hurriedly added, "Oh come now, you can't really be upset by that! I mean only, no one's a pirate anymore. I'm not saying I don't believe the story you told us – about the boat in Panama, and all that. But wouldn't it be better – better for you, I mean – to just admit that it wasn't really a case of piracy. For your information, I happen to know a little about pirates myself, and I just don't believe you're the sort to leap onto the deck of a perfectly peaceful ship and run a sailor through with your cutlass, just to teach the others to be afraid of you. Are you really going to frighten a crew of full-grown men? And thank goodness not! I don't mean to offend you – I know you don't like me to say so – but is it really so awful just to be a kid, like the rest of us?"

What Emma said, however, did appear to offend Rascal Pratt, and he said nothing for a long while. He looked out the window, as if he expected the arrival of someone. "You know, I'm not so young as you think. It's true, I'm not very big – though I'm not just a boy either, not like everyone around here thinks, anyway. But, you're right in a way – no full-grown man is ever going to be afraid of me. And I see now that pirating probably wasn't the best choice. All the same, I was in a hurry, and in truth, it kind of chose me. I don't know what to say – that's what I am."

"Goodness, you're much more than that," said Emma. "And you'll be much more than that. You've got your whole life ahead of you. You can be anything you want. You can go to school, for instance, and become a... a..."

"Yes?" said Rascal Pratt. "A what? A lighthouse keeper like your father? A painter or a schoolteacher like your mother?"

"Maybe, yes, and what's wrong with any of those? I'm sure you'd be a fine sea captain too, or any other thing you put your mind to."

Rascal Pratt shook his head. "There's nothing wrong with those. It's just... it's too late for any of that. I'm... branded, you might say. Emma – why do you suppose your father went on his little trip? I heard him talking with your mother, you know, and he didn't just go to look at schools for you. He's bringing someone back with him. Maybe your mother doesn't know what a warrant officer is, but I do. It's a policeman, a constable in the military police. That's who you are going to meet with the wagon. Your father is bringing him here."

"A constable?" said Emma with surprise. "Why would he be bringing a constable?"

Rascal Pratt started to answer several times, and finally he said, "I suppose you don't know... I'm to be arrested."

"Arrested?" cried Emma. She waited for Rascal Pratt to laugh and show that he was only teasing. But he didn't. "Whatever for? Once and for all, tell me – I won't argue anymore. You're not *really* a pirate, are you?"

"You don't have to believe me, Emma," said Rascal Pratt

shaking his head, "But, I found the gold, didn't I?"

"Of course you did – so you're a treasure hunter. And a good one, at that. But I mean, you never really attacked a ship, did you? Or killed anyone?"

A ceramic bird of Mrs. Green's decorated the windowsill. Rascal Pratt picked it up, examined it, and put it down again. "What is there to say? One fires one's weapon. One doesn't always stick around to find out."

There was a sad earnestness to what he said, and Emma looked at Rascal Pratt blankly, wondering if maybe he *had* killed a man. Could it really be possible she was alone with a killer? She thought of her father suddenly. What of him? It never occurred to her that maybe he had killed a man too. Of course, there was a difference – that was war, and Captain Green was a hero.

"Anyhow, they caught us straightaway, my brother and I," Rascal Pratt went on. "And of course, that's how I got this." He pointed to the mark of the branding iron on his face; it was rough, but recognizable as the letter P. *P is for Pirate.* It could almost be a line from a nursery rhyme, couldn't it?" He laughed darkly. "My brother was sent to Australia, on account of us being from Ireland, and still under British Rule. But because of my age, no one knew what to do with me. I've been bouncing around military prisons ever since. That's how I came to the garrison at the Presidio*, in San

---

*The Presidio is the Army base in San Francisco. It's quite famous really, and was actually founded by the Spanish in 1776, the same year as the founding of the United States. It may well have been an Ohlone village even before that. So it's been there a while. There is a military prison there too, at an old brick fort called Fort Point. Once, thirty prisoners escaped and rampaged the city of San Francisco. Only a few were ever caught. *(E.G.)*

Francisco.

"The constable there always felt bad for my case – the same one coming here with your father I'll bet, and he had heard that a British vessel was leaving San Francisco for Australia. He arranged passage for me. I left on that ship." Here, he paused again, shook his head, and looked away.

"We ran into a storm though, that first night after we left San Francisco. I hate to think I'm the Jonah, the bringer of bad luck. The ship went down, ripped her belly open on the rocks – the rocks, Emma, I'll never forget them, all jagged and black, like the broken teeth of a monster. As far as I know, I'm the only survivor. I broke my leg, I guess, in the wreckage, but I managed to get out of my irons. There had been a little dory on deck – I believe the captain was taking it to his son in Sydney as a present. It must have broken its lashings, because when I jumped overboard, there was the dory, hardly more than a child's boat, floating on the waves. I got hold of it and got myself inside. It's a miracle, really. I lay on my back, in the floor of that little boat, in the midst of the storm, thinking I'd surely come to my end. I closed my eyes and expected never to open them again. Of course, I did though, in the room right upstairs." He looked at Emma and forced a smile.

Emma was quiet for a few seconds, then an idea came to her and she said excitedly, "Rascal Pratt, I know – why don't we talk to my father?"

At this suggestion, Rascal Pratt smiled strangely – politely but sadly and turned back to the window. "No, Emma, but thank you. That won't be necessary."

"But maybe he can do something for you," Emma pressed him.

He didn't answer, and Emma laid her hand on his shoulder. "Really," she insisted, "it won't hurt to ask. My father was an officer in the Navy, you know."

Rascal Pratt flinched. Emma could feel it in her hand. He turned around slowly, and to Emma's horror, his whole face seemed to have transformed, and a glint of hot light flashed from his eyes. He glared at her for a moment or two and finally burst out angrily, "Your father? Your *father*? Yes, I know he's an officer. I know it too well! It was men like your father, Emma, who put me in prison to begin with. It was a man like your father who marked me like this!"

Emma shrank from him, utterly taken by surprise and alarmed at the change that had come over him. "No, no," she protested, "You've got it all wrong – my father's a hero! He fought in the Civil War, you know. He fought to *free* people!"

Rascal Pratt's face twisted in a sneer. "Oh, he did, did he? With brands and leg-irons, I suppose!"

More than anything it was this sarcasm that hurt Emma. She felt betrayed and was very much on the edge of tears, when an unexpected wave of wrath suddenly bubbled up from deep inside and she spat out hotly, "Well then, think what you want – and go to prison for all I care! But it's true: my father fought for *all of us!* I never said *all of us* deserved it."

The two glowered at each other in silence, until the contorted and pained expression on Rascal Pratt's face slowly faded away. It was quiet in the room again, quiet enough for Emma to hear her own angry breathing. At length, Rascal Pratt said softly, "Emma, listen, I'm sorry I said that. Of course my... my mark has nothing to do with your father. That was unfair of me. I'm sure he's a good man. But he still has rules to follow, you know. As you say, he's an officer – why, he's sworn an oath. And even if he's retired, he won't break the law for me or anyone else. He can't– and you shouldn't ask him to."

Emma said nothing. Rascal Pratt tried to catch her eye. She avoided it, and stood looking sullenly at the floor, the wall, anywhere but at him, with her arms crossed sternly in front of her. Finally he waved his hand. "Oh, Emma, it doesn't much matter, I'll be long gone before you're back with the constable. I'll leave a note thanking your parents. To tell you the truth, your mother has treated me better than anyone I can remember for a long while now. And your father, he's been good to me in his own way – I know it wasn't easy for him to have a criminal under his roof. He had every right to treat me harshly, though he never did."

Emma's heart softened a little, and she started to say something too, beginning primly with, "Well—," but not really sure how she would finish. Rascal Pratt, however, cut her off.

"No, let me finish, I just wanted to say that I owe ... I owe a lot to you Emma. To you, and Sue, and Harris of course – for pulling me into the cove to begin with. What I said before – that day on the beach, about wishing you'd just let my boat drift by – I didn't mean it. Why, I'd never have found Achilles' treasure without you. There are lots of things I'd never have done. And to think of all the other possibilities – it actually turned out quite well, when it could have been far worse." He bowed in his old-fashioned way. "So thank you, Emma Green. Rascal Pratt, at your service."

Emma felt embarrassed now, and she stammered, "N-no, it's I w-who...," still unable to think of something to say that both made sense and sounded as grown-up as this strange boy, or young man, or whoever he was.

Rascal Pratt laughed and put his hand on her shoulder. "It's all right, Emma. It is surprising, but we've both done well for ourselves, on this windswept spit of land of yours. *I* happen to know you didn't always like it here by the way, but it's growing on you nicely. Some day, perhaps we'll make a toast, to unlikely encounters in the most remote of places. I'm... in the meantime, I'm glad we part as friends." With that, he squeezed her hand, bowed again, and turned away. Emma never said good-bye. She only watched as, aided by his one crutch, he hobbled through the parlor to the front door. Where he went, she could only guess – to prepare the little dory for his departure, or maybe to some secret spot in the cypress grove to count his pieces of gold.

The Mystery of Rascal Pratt

- 12 -
The Coach Road

About four miles from Point Bonita was the road that everyone around referred to as the "coach road." Many years before, when California was still a Mexican territory, Harris Cole's great-grandfather paid laborers to build a road to his rancho. And it was still the only way into Sausalito from anywhere west of the tall hills that separated the coastal valley from the town. But the road went only as far as the Cole's, and between its farthest end and Point Bonita, there were only narrow trails that were best suited to horses, people traveling by foot, and deer. Getting the mule wagon to the road from the Point was no small undertaking, and of everyone making the trip that day – Mabel Green, Emma Green, and Emma's dog Sammy – only Sammy was excited, and he hopped happily into the wagon in beside Emma.

The weather was nice enough – the sun shone anyway. But the light had a cold, sharp glint to it, and the breeze off the ocean had already kicked up, bringing with it the smell of kelp and salt air. They had only gotten a little way up the hillside when Emma turned to look back, hoping she might get a glimpse of Rascal Pratt. He was nowhere to be seen. But not far offshore, she noticed a bank of clouds that came all the way down to the water. It was so dense that Emma almost thought it was land. That was ridiculous of course; any island that large she would have seen before.

"Fog," said her mother, looking back too and shaking her head. "I guess spring is over. They say once the summer fog comes in, everything turns cold and stays that way for months."

Of course Emma had heard talk of the famous northern California fog, but she always wondered what the fuss was about. Fog couldn't be so bad. At least it wasn't months of rain or snow. But now, looking out at the cloud that stood just offshore, she experienced a strange unease, and she fell to wringing her hands as she waited for the first bump at which she would have to hop out and start pushing.

In all, the journey took nearly three hours. Emma herself could have walked to the road in half the time. And when they got there, her hands were sore and blistered from all the lifting and straining to get the wagon over rocks and across ditches. Their mule was in a sour mood too, and even Mrs.

Green, who was normally the most cheerful member of the whole Green family, had taken to muttering, saying, "Your father was happy to walk home – why did I ever insist on meeting him?"

But finally, they were there. They came over the last hill and could see the road in the valley far below. Emma gazed upon it with relief. As they started down to it, however, she thought she heard shouting. She squinted, and there, in the road, she could see what looked like a crowd gathering. But that was impossible, way out here anyway, where there was hardly so much as a handful of people in the countryside all around. Sure enough though, some sort of commotion was in full swing, with much angry yelling and a crowd so large it must have been everyone who lived between the hills and the ocean.

Again Emma felt the uncomfortable gnawing in her stomach. Perhaps her earlier encounter with Rascal Pratt was the wrong way to start the day. Or maybe it was the fog bank that lay ominously offshore, or maybe it was the hard, bright chill in the air. Whatever it was, and now seeing the gathering at the road, Emma found herself wishing it was still yesterday – fine, sparkling, and full of adventure.

She must have twitched and fidgeted in her seat, because her mother said, "Sit still, Emma. Are you in a hurry? Whatever trouble is brewing, I certainly hope it's settled before we get there."

But the trouble was not settled by the time they reached the road. In fact it seemed to have only grown more heated. A large circle of men, and a few women too, gathered around someone Emma could not make out. One of the men was on horseback, and his horse jumped back and forth in the excitement, each time scattering other people in all directions. There was a boy on foot at the head of the horse, with his hand on the horse's bridle, and he was pushing back on the horse with all his might. Then Emma realized it wasn't just a boy – why, it was Harris! He was looking up at the man in the saddle and tears streamed down his face as he pleaded, "Please Pa! Please! A deal's a deal. You gave your word!"

Though Emma had never met Harris's father, she immediately recognized the man on horseback as Edgar Cole; and now Mr. Cole shouted at his son in return, "Out of my way, this is no business of yours!" But Harris clung to the horse's bridle harder than ever.

Emma was frightened. The horse was immense, a giant compared to Harris. She didn't know what on earth could be happening, but without waiting to find out, she leapt from the wagon and ran to the aid of her friend.

"Emma!" her mother cried. "Stop! Where are you going?"

But Emma only ran on. "Harris, Harris!" she shouted. "What's the matter? What's happening?"

Harris turned to look over his shoulder as he continued to push back on the bit of his father's horse. Mr. Cole pressed his horse on, swatting at his own son, as Harris yelled, "It's Achilles, Emma! They won't let him leave!" He pointed into the center of the crowd.

"Who won't let him leave?" cried Emma in return. "Who are 'they'?" but her voice was drowned out by a dozen others.

She didn't know what to do, especially with Harris being assailed so by his father. But she decided to leave him and push through the crowd in the direction Harris indicated. There, in the center of the ring of people, she saw Achilles, and sitting next to him was a very tired looking Sue. Achilles stood leaning on his stick and, considering the turmoil around him, he appeared very calm. But Sue did not. She sat at his feet, on the top of a wooden box, with her face hidden in her hands. Next to her was what looked like luggage – trunks and a few bags, neatly stacked at the side of the road.

"Sue!" shouted Emma as she darted between the legs of the people in the crowd. "Sue, what's the trouble? What's going on?"

Sue looked toward Emma's voice. Her dusty face was streaked with tears. "Emma?" she said unsteadily. Her voice was almost completely given over to despair. "Oh, Emma, it's awful, just awful!"

"But what is?" cried Emma.

"Well, Achilles went to speak with Harris's father last night. It was all arranged," said Sue. "Achilles paid his debt. Mr. Cole took the money, the gold Achilles offered him. He said Achilles was free to go. But this morning, Mr. Cole came to us very angry, with some papers he said he found, and he said Achilles had tricked him. Now he's trying to keep us from getting on the coach."

None of this made any sense to Emma. It had not occurred to her that the "they" which Harris spoke of – which now obviously just meant Mr. Cole – had any choice other than letting Achilles leave. And with all the gold, it made no sense that 'they' wouldn't. But most surprising to her was that Sue and Achilles were leaving so immediately – as clearly they were, for here they were at the coach road with all their bags packed. And the first question she asked was, "B-But today? Are you leaving today?"

"Oh Emma," said Sue, "I *did* want to come tell you, but then Mr. Cole got so angry. Achilles thought we should leave on the first coach, before it was too late. I really did mean to come tell you goodbye."

Emma immediately felt foolish for thinking of herself at such a moment, and she said, "Yes, of course, of course you're leaving now. Pardon me – I don't know what I was thinking. But never mind that! Why did Mr. Cole change his mind?"

Sue shook her head woefully, "I don't know. And Achilles doesn't either. He gave Mr. Cole half his gold – plus the donkey and the cart. But I guess Mr. Cole found some piece of paper that says it isn't enough."

"And so what's Achilles going to do?"

"Well, look," said Sue, pointing in her grandfather's direction with her chin. "He says he's going to get us on that coach. He says it will take the sheriff to stop us – but *I* don't want the sheriff to come! Emma, I'm afraid!"

Emma squeezed Sue's hand and tried hard to think. At that moment, there were shouts, and Emma and Sue looked up to see a number of people pointing east, toward the place where the road came round its last bend. A team of four horses had appeared, dragging behind it the coach in a cloud of red dust. It was only then Emma remembered that her father was arriving on the coach, the same coach that Sue and Achilles planned to take away. Her heart brightened and she had a momentary desire to tell Sue that they would simply ask her father what do, her father who was arriving on the coach that very instant, and he would fix everything. But the impulse seemed too familiar, and she realized she had told Rascal Pratt the very same thing, just that morning.

In just a few seconds, before Emma could say anything to Sue anyway, the coach was nearly upon them. As it approached, everyone in the crowd became quiet, with the exceptions of Mr. Cole, who continued to bellow at his son without showing any sign of concern for what might be happening around him, and also the driver of the coach, who was yelling just then to his horses.

"Whoa, Whoa!" the driver shouted to his team, and the crowd scattered out of the way. The coach rumbled to a halt. The cloud of dust subsided. There was a length of silence, and indeed, as if it were all part of a theater, the coach door opened dramatically, and out stepped Captain Green. He had a commanding air about him, as he looked with some surprise at the crowd gathered round. At first Emma couldn't put her finger on what was different about him, then she quickly realized he was dressed in his naval uniform, with its gold braids and epaulets, rather than the plain black uniform of the Lighthouse Service. The captain wrinkled his forehead and frowned, as though he assumed such a mob could only be up to no-good. Finally, after a moment or two, he caught sight of Mrs. Green with the mule and wagon. He nodded, put on his hat and descended the rest of the way from the coach, and then turned to retrieve his baggage from the driver who was handing it down from the carriage's roof.

Emma let go of Sue's hand and ran to her father. "Papa, Papa!" she shouted. "You've got to help!" But before she reached him, another man stepped down from the coach. He too was wearing a military uniform, but from the Army rather than the Navy. Emma abruptly stopped. She remembered now what Rascal Pratt had told her. Could this be the constable, the warrant officer in the military police? Had her father really brought someone to arrest Rascal Pratt?

"Emma!" exclaimed Captain Green, obviously not expecting to find his own daughter keeping company with such a crowd. "What's going on here?"

Emma could not take her eyes off the man her father had brought with him. Without answering Captain Green, she backed away from him and into the center of the circle where Achilles and Sue waited with their bags. Her father put down his own bag and followed. The crowd made way for him.

As he stepped past the last few onlookers and into the middle of the innermost ring, Emma said, "Mr. Cole broke his promise." She spoke very plainly, and not particularly loudly. Her eyes were still on her father's guest, and in her voice was a strange seriousness, as though she were reporting something to a public official rather than own father, someone with the power to change things, but from whom she suddenly expected very little. "He took Achilles' money and now he won't let him go."

A hush descended over the crowd. Even Mr. Cole had stopped his shouting now that Captain Green stood there on the side of the road in his uniform. As for Captain Green though, he looked very ill at ease. And while he did follow Emma to the center of the circle, Emma could see in his eyes that he wished he were not there. He looked at Achilles leaning calmly on his stick. He looked at Sue sitting on her box in the dust. And he looked up at Harris's father sitting on his horse. Then he turned to Emma and said, "But sweetheart, we have nothing to do with this. It's none of our business."

When the people in the crowd heard this, they began to shout again, nearly everyone at once. Cries of "You see, he has no say!" could be heard on one side. Cries of "For shame!" could be heard on the other. And above all could be heard Mr. Cole, who had begun to shout at Harris anew, crying "For the last time, boy, get out of my way!"

Emma turned to her father and pulled hard on his cuff to stop him from leaving. "But, Papa, we must do something. Achilles already bought his rights. He's free to go. And now Mr. Cole has changed the price. It's not fair!"

The clamor from the crowd was so loud that Emma could hardly hear her own words. Captain Green held up his hand to quiet those around him. But when no one in the crowd heeded him, he bellowed, "Silence!" and all at once, it became quiet again on the coach road, so quiet that the only thing to be heard was the gravel under Captain Green's boots as he approached Mr. Cole and his horse.

"I'm afraid we haven't had the pleasure of meeting," said the captain as pleasantly as could be expected, considering the circumstances. "My name is John Green, I'm the new—"

"Yes, yes, the new lighthouse keeper," said Mr. Cole with a sneer. "I know who you are. But you were right the first time – this *is* none of your business. So unless you know something about these sorts of matters, I suggest you attend to your wicks and lanterns. I've got papers right here, and Achilles, *Mr. Achilles*, is not yet free to leave. He cheated me out of my money and I happen to know he's got more. I want the rest of it, the rest of the gold he has in that box!"

At this, a murmur ran through the crowd. Captain Green looked at Achilles oddly and said, "Gold?"

Achilles said nothing and made no movement of any sort.

But Mr. Cole said, "You heard right, gold. His grand-daughter is sitting on a box of it. Last night when Achilles came to talk to me, he said he was giving me all he could afford. And I took it. Good riddance, I thought. I was tired of letting the old man live on my farm for nothing, for *charity*. But now I seen what's in that box. It's gold – and a lot more of it. So I read the contract. Mr. Achilles can only pay off his debt to the rancho with *labor*. He ain't yet, he never will, and anything in his possession is legally *mine*."

Before Captain Green had a chance to respond, Achilles

spoke. It was the first time he had said anything since Emma had arrived. And in a clear and steady voice, he said, "I did not trick you. I gave you what I could afford. I'm an old man, I'm nearly blind, and I cannot work. I need the rest to support myself, now that I am free, since I am free, since I will get on that stage coach whether you like it or not. I need the rest of my gold – yes it's *gold* – to support my granddaughter, to send her to school. It's my duty as her grandfather and guardian, and I am bound to keep it."

These words seemed to incense Mr. Cole like hot coals, and he writhed in his saddle. "Don't talk to me about duty!" he roared. "You don't need so much money to perform your duty! You can live in a *shack* with just a dollar or two. Do you think you're better than everyone else? *Duty* – now, that's something that should cost you dearly. I lost the use of my right knee fighting Indians, you know – that was my duty! And anyway, I've got your papers right here, and it says you can't leave until I agree that your debt is paid! It's all nice and legal – it's California law!"

There was a momentary silence. Captain Green took the opportunity to whisper to Emma, "Come on, honey, this is between them. We have to go now."

It was very much as Emma had feared. But in truth, she was bewildered. Wasn't this all about the same thing he had fought for in the Civil War? Certainly that's what he had told her during the war – every time he had to leave the family to put to sea. And she said, "But, Papa, it's not *fair*. Achilles is my friend. Sue is my friend. They just want what's theirs. They even paid for it. *You* told me everyone has the right to live free of the yoke of others. That's what you said!"

Captain Green looked uncomfortably around him. He didn't reply for a few moments. Finally he said, "Emma, this is not a war. This is not a fighting matter. I'm a lighthouse keeper now, not a policeman. And besides, this is for a judge to decide. What Achilles needs is a lawyer."

"Well, then, let's get him one!" Emma snapped.

Captain Green sighed. He looked at the people in the crowd. He looked at his guest, the constable from the military police. And he looked at his own wife, Mrs. Green, who waited up the hill. Every one of them seemed keenly interested in what he would do. But he only took Emma by the shoulders and said, "We'll see. For now, I've other business. Please get in the wagon."

Emma, however, dug her feet into the ground.

"Emma," pleaded Captain Green, "I promise, I'll see what we can do. But we have to go about it the right way. Right now though, I have Sergeant Cathgart here, and we're in a bit of a hurry."

Emma could hardly see through her tears. "A hurry?" she shouted angrily. "I know what your other business is, you know! I know why you're in a hurry. Well, you're too late – Rascal Pratt already left. He left this morning!"

Emma was alarmed and frightened that she would ever talk to her father in this way. But to her further dismay, it turned out that she was not completely correct in what she had said. For just then, she heard the sort of sound that grabs your attention no matter what you are doing. It was the sound of money – solid, heavy money, falling over itself with a *clink-clink-clink*.

She turned around slowly. The crowd went quiet again. The eyes of everyone in it were fixed on the ground under the feet of Mr. Cole's horse. For there, in the dirt, lay a handful of gold coins. And it was clear from the whispers that ran through the onlookers that few among them had ever seen

Spanish doubloons. And at the edge of the crowd, leaning on a crutch, was Rascal Pratt.

Emma's heart sank. Why was he here? He was supposed to be far away. She spun around to look at the constable. She saw that he had come to attention too and was looking at the boy with great interest. Emma felt certain he knew exactly who Rascal Pratt was. In fact, there even seemed to be a smile growing on his lips.

For his part, Rascal Pratt could not have failed to see the constable. Even so, on his one crutch, he hobbled a step closer to the crowd. His hurt leg seemed to cause him some pain. Emma wondered how far he had walked.

He paused to rest on his crutch, and as he did, he said loudly, "How much will it take?" It was completely silent. Not a soul answered him. He took another step. "I said, how much will it take, Mr. Cole?"

"How much will *what* take?" said Mr. Cole scornfully as he moved his horse a few steps sideways to get a better look at the coins on the ground.

"How much will it take to buy this man's freedom?"

"What's it to you, boy?" laughed Mr. Cole. "Certainly more than a few pieces of gold, if it's any business of yours."

"Certainly more than a few pieces indeed," said Rascal Pratt. "Who ever thought less? So then, what's the exact figure? I want you to name the price."

"That's between me and the Indian," snapped Mr. Cole. "I don't discuss business with children."

At this, Rascal Pratt only smiled. And with his crutch, he took another step, and then another. He didn't stop until he was in front of Mr. Cole's horse. Harris moved out of his way. Rascal Pratt reached out and caught the reins where they hung down under the horse's neck. He looked up at Mr.

Cole with an apologetic smile and then, in one quick movement, he snatched the reins so hard that they came right out
of the man's hands.

"*I've* got the rest of the gold," said Rascal Pratt before
Mr. Cole could say a word. "I helped Achilles find it and now
I'm acting as his agent. If you can tell me exactly how much
you want, I'm prepared to talk to Achilles and give it to you.
But this time, you'll have to give me an exact figure. And
you'll have to give up that piece of paper you've been waving
about."

It seemed to take a moment or two for the meaning of
these words to sink in, but after a few seconds the smirk on
Mr. Cole's mouth widened until his lips curled with anger.
It really started to appear that he didn't care how much gold
he had or how much he could get – his meanness had got
the better of him, and now he was determined only that the
blind old man, Achilles, should never have his freedom.

"How much?" he cried. "How much? How much is a
man's life worth? You tell me, boy! Why, it would take *double* what he already gave me. Double, and not a penny less!"
He tilted his head back to the sky, and showing many rotten
teeth, he laughed such a hideous cackle that it filled the valley and echoed back off the hillsides as though a chorus of
demons had joined him.

Rascal Pratt waited patiently. When Mr. Cole's laughing
came to an end and he had wiped his mouth, Rascal Pratt
said very matter-of-factly, "Very well, double – I'll see to it
that you get it."

"What?" gasped Mr. Cole. His eyes darted between
Rascal Pratt and Achilles. "Double?" he said, as if he couldn't
have heard right.

At this though, Sue cried, "No, Rascal Pratt, don't! Please

don't."

And Achilles, too, said, "Not to this man. He's been paid far too much already for something that was never his."

Rascal Pratt looked over to them. Though he said nothing, and certainly didn't plead, he appeared to ask them for something. At length, Achilles nodded.

Rascal Pratt turned back to Mr. Cole. "Give the papers to Captain Green," he said, "and I'll tell you where you'll find your gold. It's not far, and it's exactly double."

Mr. Cole hesitated. Then, from his coat pocket, he withdrew a bundle of papers which, by their looks, were quite ancient. Very slowly, he handed the papers to Captain Green, and as he did, he gestured with them toward Rascal Pratt, snarling, "If that boy is lying, Captain, you give these right back."

"As we agreed, this was none of my business," said Captain Green sternly. "But you realize, by handing these papers over to me, you are making the matter my personal affair. I will see to it that each of you holds to his word." As he spoke, he thumbed through the bundle. Suddenly he stopped. "Why, they're in Spanish," he marveled, in scarcely more than a whisper, "–and signed almost a hundred years ago." And looking at Achilles in wonder, he asked, "Can you really be that old?"

Achilles turned toward the sound of the captain's voice. Indeed, his face was streaked with years of work and sun. Emma thought it very handsome. He nodded and said quietly, "It does seem a very long time, doesn't it?"

But Mr. Cole interrupted impatiently. "Enough of this pilavering! Where's my gold?"

"Please, Pa," pleaded Harris.

Mr. Cole's eyes flashed at his son and he shouted, "Just

tell me where the gold is! Where is it?" He worked himself quite nearly into a fit, and Emma thought he would fall out of his saddle.

With his crutch Rascal Pratt pointed over the hill, to the south. "It's hidden in that little cove, just beyond the hill, in the bottom of my dory. I hadn't meant to deliver you an entire boatload of gold, you know. I actually came to say goodbye to Achilles and Sue. And to your son too – he's my friend, you'll be pleased to know. But, the gold is there and now that you know where it is, even you will find it. I'd come with you, but I think my leg won't make it." And with that, he threw the reins of the horse back to Mr. Cole, adding "But hurry, before someone else beats you to it. It is just sitting there, after all."

From his saddle, Mr. Cole looked down at the faces in the crowd. They were mostly people who worked for him maybe a neighbor or two. He had known every one of them his whole life. Yet, a look of suspicion crept into his eyes as he turned from face to face. Last of all, he looked down at his son. The two gazed wordlessly at one another for what seemed an eternity. But then the elder Cole's hand began to creep along the horse's mane until they reached the reins. He hesitated, then wrenched his eyes away from his son's, and spinning his horse about, he galloped off in the direction Rascal Pratt had pointed.

The Mystery of Rascal Pratt

- 13 -
As P is to D

The following day the fog came in. Emma woke to the drip-drip-drip of water trickling off the roof one drop at a time. At first she thought it was raining. But when she got up and looked out her window, she saw that a low, thick cloud covered the world outside with fine droplets. A chill breeze off the ocean sent shivers through everything, even the bushes outside the window.

Emma rubbed her eyes and looked toward the cove. And there she saw what she dreaded, a sailing vessel. Emma recognized it – it was Lieutenant Walker's lighthouse tender. He was the young, ambitious officer who had first brought them their supplies for the fog cannon, many weeks before. He brought supplies again today, but that wasn't the only reason he had anchored in the cove.

The day before, on the way home from the coach road, Captain Green had made Emma sit up front between himself and Mrs. Green. In the back rode Sergeant Cathgart and Rascal Pratt. Rascal Pratt wore wrist-irons. It was very quiet on the front bench, but in back, the sergeant and Rascal Pratt chattered away like old friends. Every time Emma turned around to listen, her father nudged her, saying, "Turn around, Emma."

However, at one point, she heard Rascal Pratt say, "Sergeant, if I may ask, why didn't you just take me back on the coach?"

"Because I expected to find you at Point Bonita," said the sergeant. "And a launch has already been sent there to fetch us."

"A launch sent for me?" said Rascal Pratt. "Why, I'm honored."

"And you should be," said Sergeant Cathgart, "though to tell you the truth, it's the same launch that brings supplies to the lighthouse. Let me think – it's the *Eucalyptus,* I believe, which is under Lieutenant Walker's command. If I'm not mistaken, he's bringing more powder for Captain Green's fog gun."

At this, Captain Green, for all his telling Emma not to

listen, twisted around and said, "What? More powder?"

"Why, yes," said Sergeant Cathgart, "I believe Lieutenant Walker has a whole boatload of the stuff."

"I don't doubt it," muttered Captain Green, "but I simply ordered butter..."

And so it was that now, the next morning, Emma woke to see Lieutenant Walker's cutter, the *Eucalyptus*, anchored in the cove. As she stared out the window, she thought of her friends. Sue and Achilles would be in San Francisco by now. And Rascal Pratt had slept on a cold, musty cot, under guard and locked in one of the storage rooms at the lighthouse. But it was Harris, poor Harris, for whom her heart went out most. He had returned to his father's house, she supposed, and there was no telling how much trouble he had caught.

Emma pulled herself away from the window and got dressed quickly. She hurried downstairs and out the front door of the house without saying good-morning, even to her mother. Sammy got up though and followed her out, trotting beside her as she made her way down the path toward the lighthouse. She wanted to check on Rascal Pratt as soon as she could. He was such a hardy sort that she doubted a night on a cot in the dreary basement of the lighthouse would have affected him much; still, she hoped they were at least giving him breakfast.

But when she got to the tunnel, which was just about the halfway point between the main house and the lighthouse, she found the iron tunnel door not only closed, but also locked. Quite unexpectedly, all the anger inside her came rushing out, and she kicked the metal door hard with her toe. She was wearing a pair of older, uncomfortable shoes, her new ones having been lost in the ocean. Luckily for her though, the old ones were still plenty sturdy – otherwise she would have hurt herself. The door, for its part, remained firmly shut. Emma kicked it once more, and then shoved her hands into her pockets with a disgusted "*harrumph!*" A low wooden fence ran along the edge of the path, and feeling very much defeated, Emma leaned back against it.

Presently, she heard a creaking sound. The handle of the iron door turned and out stepped Emma's father. He seemed surprised to see Emma waiting at the entrance, but he smiled and said, "So that was you banging!"

Emma didn't answer. She only glowered at him, and then leaned forward to peer into the tunnel. But Captain Green closed the iron door behind him and locked it.

He then turned and joined her at the fence, putting his hands on the top railing. He looked out over the cove, while Emma looked the other way, at the big, blank cliff which the tunnel disappeared into. After a few minutes Captain Green said, "Emma, I know you're not happy with me. I know he's become your friend. Maybe I was wrong to not prevent that from happening. But you have to consider everyone's situation – not just your friend's – and you should consider it from the point of view of the law. The law is much bigger than any of us, and the truth is, your friend has gotten himself onto the wrong side of it. He, and he alone, can answer for that. He's going to prison, today, and there's nothing any of us can do about it. Believe me, it's much better that he be under the protection of Sergeant Cathgart than hunted down by someone else. Still, the sergeant is taking him – *Mr. Pratt* – away, just as soon as the tide comes around."

Now, Emma could admit to herself that she didn't understand the law. She didn't know what it meant when people talked about how "big" it was. But she did know that not once in her whole life had she ever seen or heard her father being so unkind. To Emma, the only crime Rascal Pratt had committed – that of trying to live up to some ridiculous idea about becoming a pirate by stealing a pleasure yacht – it just seemed so unimportant. Maybe he had wielded a gun somewhere along the line. *Maybe.* And in a fit of anger, she said, "Papa, it doesn't even matter to you what he's done. You've never liked him from the day he got here. Why, it offends you just to say his name!"

"To say his name?" repeated Captain Green with a frown. "Not to say it, no. If I said his name strangely, it's only because...," But the captain's voice trailed off and he seemed uncertain how to finish his thought.

"Only because what?" Emma demanded. "You don't want me being friends with someone who's going to jail? Well, I don't care about that – I know him, Papa, and even if he did try to steal someone's boat, he's still much better and braver than many people I know!"

The captain sighed. "No doubt, Emma, no doubt he is. He's not a bad sort and I never thought he was." He looked at his daughter wearily, then said, "Emma, I'm going to tell you a story. Perhaps you don't know, but for the last two days I have been in San Francisco, at the Presidio. There's an army garrison there, a prison of sorts. I've been looking through the records, the records of a group of prisoners who left San Francisco on a British ship about two months ago. The ship was bound for Australia. And, as it turns out, there was a boy on that ship, a young man, sixteen years old. He had an ugly scar on his face and bragged among other things, of being a pirate. He might have had a nickname, in the manner of ruffians and hooligans, but according to the records, his name was *Roscoe Pratt.*"

"*Roscoe*," repeated Emma with a tender smile. "That's a nice name. I always wondered what his real name was. And Rascal is a very nice nickname if you ask me, even if *you* don't like it."

Her father nodded patiently, but went on with his story. "Perhaps, perhaps. But, as I was saying, this boy left San Francisco about two months ago, a little less, on a British prison ship, the *Gamma*, bound for Hobart, Australia, on the island of Tasmania. He never got there. The *Gamma* sank shortly after it left San Francisco, not far off shore. Maybe you remember the storm – we had been here at Point Bonita only a few days. The storm sent the ship onto the rocks near the Farallon Islands*, about twenty miles out." He pointed west over his shoulder with his thumb. "There were no survivors, everyone on board was presumed drowned." He turned sideways to look at Emma.

"Everyone but one," murmured Emma, almost proudly. And looking at her father, she said, "Papa, I heard this story already. I guess I should have told you. It's funny though, I believed most of it, but for some reason I never could believe

---

*The Farallon Islands are a little group of rocky islands due west of the city of San Francisco, about twenty-four miles out in the Pacific Ocean. On a clear day you can see them from here, and even from parts of San Francisco. I still remember the first time I saw them. I was greatly astonished – for there they were one day, poking up over the horizon. The Indians called them "The Islands of the Dead" and left them alone. I've heard it was once a paradise for animals – seals, birds, and all sorts of other living things. Then seal hunters from New England and also from Russia killed most of the seals. These days, in 1866 that is, there is a company which goes to the islands to collect the eggs of the sea birds that nest there, and then sells the eggs in San Francisco. Between them and the seal hunters, the wildlife on the islands has not done particularly well. *(E.G.)*

he was actually sixteen years old. I should have. He told the truth, it turns out."

Captain Green nodded gently. He looked back out over the cove and said, "Well, don't be too hard on yourself, Emma, for not believing everything you hear. You see, Roscoe Pratt was *not* the youngest prisoner aboard that ship. There was another boy, around fourteen or so. Very small for his age, this other fellow. Fourteen years old, but everyone I talked to said he looked much younger."

Emma stepped away from the rail when he said this and she turned to face him. She got an odd feeling in her stomach and her knees felt unexpectedly wobbly. "I-I don't understand," she said. "Who was he, the other boy?"

Captain Green shrugged. "No one knows, not exactly. No one knew his real name and the boy himself would never say. He only used invented names titles usually, obviously made up, inventions of a fanciful mind – so-and-so the Red, the Black, the Rogue – things of that sort. They say he was a serious lad, seldom smiled, hardly ever happy. And who would be, having spent much of his life in prison?

"He seemed to know about boats, and there's some thought, from his accent, that he was Scottish or maybe from Ireland, perhaps of a family of fishermen. He said nothing

155

about his past, even when he was defending himself in court. He too had a scar on his right cheek, though not a sabre cut, like that of Roscoe Pratt. No, his was a brand, a brand from a hot iron, in the shape of a letter. On this, at least, the record is quite clear."

"But what was he doing at the Presidio?" asked Emma, both her mind and her heart now racing, "And why did they put him on a prison ship for Australia?"

"That's a good question," said her father. "To the best I can tell, it was simply a way of getting rid of him. Somehow, maybe from Roscoe Pratt himself, this young lad heard about the British boat and began telling everyone that he too had a brother in Australia, and he wanted to go on the ship. The Army had no interest in keeping him – who wants to keep a child in jail, after all? I imagine it was cheaper to pay the captain of the prison ship to take him on board."

"But why was he at the Presidio in the first place?" said Emma. "Why were they holding him there?"

"Silly things, like you say. Petty things. Repeated crimes like the theft of a can of beans or a side of bacon. Escape. Attempted escape. Insubordination. He was never discharged as a soldier and now everything he does just piles up on him. His sentences in military prison only get longer and longer."

"So it all started with a can of beans," said Emma sadly, "and he ended up stealing a yacht. He *is* just a thief, then. A common thief. A street urchin. And for that, they branded him."

Captain Green narrowed his eyes suddenly and squinted at his daughter. "Emma, you don't know what that brand on his face means, do you?"

"Of course I do," said Emma. "It means he's a pirate. They branded him because he tried to steal a yacht which happened to belong to an officer in the U.S. Navy."

Captain Green looked at her blankly for some time, then slowly shook his head. "I see. I suppose that's what he told you. Well, Emma, he's not a pirate. The brand means he's a deserter."

"A deserter?" repeated Emma. She had heard this word before, but not recently, not since the war. Towards the end of the Civil War, however, she remembered grown-ups using it frequently. If she understood it correctly, a deserter was someone too afraid to fight. And Emma said with a scoff, "You mean a soldier who quit? A coward?" No sooner had she said this than she laughed. "Rascal Pratt is no coward! He's the bravest person I know! You saw him with Mr. Cole. Besides, he's too young to be a soldier."

Again Captain Green nodded as though he agreed with her. "I didn't say he was a coward, Emma, and knowing what I know of him, I never would. But during the war, the battles were more terrible than you can imagine, and I don't blame a person, anyone, for wanting to walk away. And there were many boy soldiers. I won't horrify you with the stories. But picture hell on earth, if you can – and you can't, unless you can imagine all the horrible things one man can do to another – and there you have a pretty good idea of it. Men – boys – marched straight into cannon fire, knowing they didn't stand a chance, knowing they would be blown to bits, even seeing the men ahead of them mown down, heads blown clean off or their whole bodies reduced to bloody pieces – Emma, I'm sorry to put it that way, but that's not the half of it. You just don't know what the engines of war, the engines of man, can do to flesh and blood. Do you call someone a coward who walks away from this? And your friend isn't even American – what on earth would motivate him to fight? He probably just got mixed up in the war because he was poor and came to this country to find work. Many's the boy who fought and died in that war, it makes me sad to say. All the same, I think a young boy can be forgiven for not wanting to fight. I believe a boy can even be forgiven for being *afraid* to fight."

"So why wasn't he then?" said Emma, who was struggling to hold back tears, "Why *isn't* he forgiven?"

Captain Green sighed deeply. "Well, people have strong feelings about it, Emma. And the brand is a mark that's particularly hard for people to forgive, especially if they lost someone who didn't run. It's the mark of shame.

"Usually, the punishment for deserters was death, you know. But a dead man, or dead boy, can't fight anymore, and we needed soldiers. So, we resorted to the practice of branding. Both sides did. We thought it the *perfect* punishment – the deserted could be sent back out to battle, and if he died, so much the better, one less bullet the rest of us had to worry about. And if he survived, well, he would still have the punishment, the shame of the brand, forever.

"Even if he leaves the country, your friend, returns to Ireland, or wherever he's from, he'll always have that mark on his face. Rumors will spread, and chances are, people will find out what it means. Years from now even, whenever anyone looks at him, they'll see the mark branded into his flesh and it will be hard for them not to think, 'Here's a man who ran from battle. Here's a man who left his friends. Here's a coward!' For any man, young or old, a coward is about the worse thing one could possibly be. Yet when people see that D, that's what they'll think, even though they might never be called on to face the cannons themselves."

Emma had listened despondently to this whole explanation. But now she lifted her head hopefully, and said, "The letter *D*? Did you say *D*? But Rascal Pratt has a *P* on his face!"

Captain Green put his hands tenderly on his daughter's shoulders. "Emma, don't you see? That's what this is all about. He *changed* it. He changed his *D* to a *P*. This boy, call him Rascal Pratt if you like, was marked for life as a coward. And when the real Roscoe Pratt died in the shipwreck, your friend borrowed the name and re-branded himself as a pirate. He carved the *P* into his own face! He carved it on top of the *D*, with a knife, to cover it up. Presto – he was Rascal Pratt, the famous pirate. I imagine he came up with the plan sometime before and thought maybe he'd do it when he got to Australia, to start fresh. But when Roscoe Pratt died, the real Roscoe Pratt, someone who actually *was* accused of piracy – on paper and everything – your friend Rascal realized he had an opportunity. I think he tried to change the letter when he was adrift in his rowboat." Captain Green bent to look into his daughter's face. "I'm sorry Emma. I know he's your friend, and in a strange way, I wanted you to keep believing what he told you. But, if it makes you feel any better, you are right about one thing, he's certainly no coward. I just hope he knows that too."

Emma found herself softly crying. It wasn't so much that she felt her friend had lied to her, had tricked her. Instead, she felt that, like Rascal Pratt, the truth had simply caught up with her and she was no longer able to escape it. After a while, she looked up at her father and said, "So what *is* going to happen to him?"

"I don't know," said Captain Green. "Sergeant Cathgart is fond of him and will see to it that he's treated well. I suppose he'll end up back at the Presidio. Or maybe the new military prison they're building on Alcatraz Island, in the middle of the bay."

159

"Forever, I bet," said Emma forlornly, as she looked down at the cove.

"Not forever," said her father, "but for a long time."

- 14 -

Changing of the Guard

The tide was running hard now out of the cove and the cutter tugged on its anchor. The fog was blowing thicker too, but not so thick that Emma couldn't see the men as they worked on the cutter's deck, lowering barrel after barrel of powder into a small rowboat that floated tethered at the larger boat's side. She stood next to her father, just outside the tunnel, on the path overlooking the cove. Neither had moved for sometime; neither had spoken.

After a long, long while, Emma asked, though she knew it was futile, "Can't I just go in to say goodbye?"

Captain Green didn't answer at first. At length though, he heaved a sigh and said, "No, Emma, I'm sorry, but you may not. Whatever you think of him, he's quite keen to escape and I don't want you out at the lighthouse adding to the confusion. It's hard enough already, you know – neither the sergeant nor I like keeping the boy in chains."

Just then, a man appeared on the path not far from them. Emma looked up and recognized Lieutenant Walker, and Captain Green turned to face the approaching man.

"Richard," the captain greeted him with a nod, for that was the other officer's first name.

"John," said Lieutenant Walker with a frown, returning the greeting and the nod as well.

"Tell me, Richard," said Captain Green, "is that a new gun you have on the foredeck of your cutter there?"

"Why yes," said the younger officer proudly. "It's a nine-pounder. Fully rifled. I just had it mounted."

"I see. And what is it for?"

"Well, I'm sure it will come in handy. My father asked me to test it out. As you recall, he owns a share of an armaments manufactory. And there's talk of a war brewing, with Paraguay."

"Paraguay, of course," said Captain Green. "I always suspected. Well, it's sure to be a rout. I suppose you intend to fight this time?"

Lieutenant Walker's face turned crimson. He sucked down his breath indignantly and said, "I certainly will, if called upon."

Captain Green chuckled. "I'm only teasing, Richard. It's just that, you're in the Lighthouse Service, and your boat is to supply lighthouses. It's humorous, that's all, to see a gun used for that!"

The younger officer however did not take the teasing so jovially. His face was flushed all the way down to his wool collar, and he replied stiffly, "Joke if you like, but when I come across the enemy, I'll be ready. Now, if you'll excuse me, I need access through this tunnel. We have your powder."

From not far away came the sound of grunts and strains and the slipping of boots on gravel. The men of Lieutenant Walker's crew were nearing the top of the trail from the cove with their first load of gunpowder.

"Carefully, now, carefully!" Lieutenant Walker shouted to his men. Turning back to Captain Green, he said, "Ah, here it is now   your monthly supply." He took a step closer to Captain Green and in a hushed and almost apologetic tone, he added, "By the way, John, I looked in your magazine, below the lighthouse, and it seems you haven't used any powder at all since the last delivery." He arched an eyebrow.

"In the first place, Richard, what you are calling a 'magazine' is really just a basement," said Captain Green, who did not speak in hushed tones at all. "And today is the first truly foggy day since... since your last visit, come to think of it. So, correct, I haven't fired the fog cannon once."

"Nevertheless, John," said Lieutenant Walker, "some of the powder is intended to keep you and your crew in practice."

"My crew?" laughed Captain Green. "You mean my family, I suppose."

Lieutenant Walker shrugged. "If you prefer, yes." He turned to look back again towards his men. "Anyway, this powder is expensive, John, and my father is paying for it. If you aren't going to use it, I'll take it to someone who will."

"So much the better," said Captain Green. "In fact, the load you have there on the wagon is more than enough to get me through the summer. There's no need to unload the rest from your boat. I won't use it and I don't like having it."

"All right then," sniffed Lieutenant Walker. "We'll get out of your cove as soon as the tide comes around." He looked at a gold watch that he took from his pocket. "That's two hours from now."

"Or, an hour and a half, at least by my reckoning," said Captain Green looking at a watch of his own. "I don't know if you've been reading about the recent developments in tide prediction*..."

Lieutenant Walker waved his hand. "As I said, roughly two hours. Now, what about that deserter you caught? Is he bound and ready for transport?"

Captain Green glanced awkwardly at Emma. "Yes... I believe he is." He took a key from his pocket as though to open the tunnel door, but then stopped and turned to his daughter. "Emma, why don't you run up the trail towards the house. I don't want you near the powder when they bring it through the tunnel."

When Emma opened her mouth to protest, her father leaned toward her and added in a low voice, "Don't worry,

---

*It has always been known that tides follow the orbit of the moon around the earth, more or less. But it wasn't until this very year, 1866, that the English scientist Sir William Thomson (also known as Lord Kelvin) came up with a new method for the prediction of tides which he called *harmonic analysis*. The principle that Sir William Thomson uses was also discussed by the ancient Greeks two thousand years ago, but it wasn't until Thomson's work that it became usable. *(E.G.)*

when I bring him out, I'll make sure you get to tell him good-bye. Now, here come these buffoons with their precious powder – be quick and get up the hill as far as you can."

Emma obeyed. She and Sammy trotted up the path past the place where it forked down to the cove. They gave a wide berth to the men and their wagon, who were just then taking a break. Several men stood around the wagon, mopping their foreheads. And several more actually sat on the wagon, casually using the kegs of powder as backrests. Emma shuddered and ran on.

When she was clear of the men and the powder, and a distance of twenty or so yards beyond them on the path, she turned around to watch. Captain Green gave Lieutenant Walker the go-ahead, and he in turn whistled to his men and beckoned them on. "Carefully now! Steady, steady," he said as they made their way with the wagon to the tunnel, which Captain Green had opened for them.

The wagon carrying the powder was almost as large as the opening to the tunnel itself. The men in the crew spent several minutes lining up their cart so as not to bump the tunnel walls. It seemed no one wanted to go into the tunnel with so large a load of explosives. But Lieutenant Walker drove them in like sheep, waving in the air, not a walking stick, but actually a sword in its scabbard, which, though quite unusual for the skipper of a lighthouse tender, he always seemed to have fastened on his belt. All of a sudden, though, the progress halted. There was much yelling and confusion. Then, from between the tops of the kegs of powder and the roof of the tunnel, out scampered Rascal Pratt himself. His wrists were bound in irons and chained to cuffs around his ankles; still he clambered over the barrels as if they held only wheat or water. Once outside, he waited patiently at the iron door for

Sergeant Cathgart, who edged gingerly between the wagon and the tunnel wall.

"What is the meaning of this?" barked Lieutenant Walker. He then looked closely at Rascal Pratt and exclaimed, "Stop – you can't mean this is the deserter? Why, he's only a boy."

"That's right, Richard," said Captain Green, "I'm sorry he's not the threat you hoped for."

But after a momemt or two, a cruel smile crept across Lieutenant Walker's face and replaced the confused expression that had been there a second before. "On the contrary," he said, "he'll do nicely. I'm sure I can make him talk."

At this, Sergeant Cathgart, who until then had been dusting off his uniform, looked up with a start and interjected, "Talk? About what?"

"Oh, things," said the lieutenant. "Other deserters, for starters. Where there's one, there're bound to be more. They travel in gangs, as everyone knows."

"The war is over, Lieutenant." said Sergeant Cathgart. "This boy was charged with desertion two years ago, and he's been punished for it already, as you can see from the mark on his face. Now he's imprisoned on charges of theft. That's all. He was caught stealing food. And books."

"Yes, but he's also an escaped convict."

"Nothing of the sort!" retorted the sergeant. "A prison-ship wrecked – no fault of this boy's. And he survived. I don't see how that makes him an escaped convict! Besides, it isn't the job of the Lighthouse Service—"

"But he didn't turn himself in, either," said Lieutenant Walker, not letting the sergeant complete his sentence. He tapped his chin thoughtfully. "As with all things regarding the law, we have only to think creatively. And let us not forget the public. The public wants to be assured that all these...

cowards have been fully punished." To the men in his crew, he instructed, "Take the prisoner away. Straight to the brig."

"The brig, sir?" said one of the sailors. "But, there's no brig aboard our boat."

"Then stuff him in a sail locker!" snarled Lieutenant Walker. "As for the rest of you, get this powder unloaded!"

"A sail locker won't be necessary, Skipper," said Sergeant Cathgart. "I'll be on board to watch him."

Lieutenant Walker turned to look more closely at Sergeant Cathgart. He smiled politely and raised a finger. "Say, Sergeant, I'm afraid there's been some sort of mix-up. We actually don't have room for both you and the prisoner. Yes, a mix-up. As you can see, she's not a large ship."

"I'll stand the whole way then, holding onto the rigging if I have to," said Sergeant Cathgart. "He's my prisoner, after all, and I have my orders."

"I'm the captain of the ship!" cried Lieutenant Walker in an impatient outburst which took nearly everyone by surprise, not least for the veins it caused to protrude suddenly from his forehead. He collected his composure, and smoothed the breast of his jacket. "And what I say, goes."

Sergeant Cathgart continued to protest and he stepped up to block the path, putting himself between Rascal Pratt and the men of Lieutenant Walker's crew. Just then there came a very quiet rattle of iron chain, so quiet that even Emma might not have noticed, except the sergeant paused and glanced at Rascal Pratt. Emma followed his glance just in time to notice something flit across the boy's face, a smile perhaps, or something similar. The sergeant looked to Captain Green, who nodded, though with only the slightest inclination of his head.

"Very well," said the sergeant. "But I should warn you, once he leaves my custody, he's your responsibility. Completely."

Lieutenant Walker dismissed the warning with a wave. "You may accompany him down to the water, Sergeant, but don't trouble yourself beyond that. The prisoner will arrive at the Presidio in one piece." He chuckled darkly.

For a while, Emma lingered on the path to the house. A sailor from the crew of the cutter led Sergeant Cathgart and Rascal Pratt towards the cove. In the meantime, Captain Green turned his attention back to the rest of Lieutenant Walker's crew, who seemed to have gotten stuck in the tunnel with their load of powder.

Seeing this, Emma glanced up the path toward the main house, where, no doubt her father intended for her to return during the transfer of the gunpowder. She looked at the tunnel, and then, taking advantage of the distraction there, she stole back down the path, to the place where it met the cove trail, and fell into line behind the sailor, the sergeant, and Rascal Pratt.

When they reached the cove, Emma could make out the cutter more easily. Billows of mist blew in from around the point and seemed almost to roll down the bluffs. White-capped waves that formed on the bay now rolled into the cove and broke in ragged lines on the beach just a few yards beyond the spot where the little company halted. The sailor from Lieutenant Walker's crew put two fingers to his mouth and whistled.

Looking out to the boat, Emma could just barely see another crewman. The sailor on shore beckoned a few times and finally the man on the boat seemed to get his meaning. He lowered himself into a rowboat which had been bumping at the stern of the cutter and began rowing towards shore. The rowboat was nearly swept all the way down to the point by the current, but the man rowing battled it, and after some time he managed to get the boat close to the little landing. He turned it with one oar and ran it up onto the pebble beach.

Sergeant Cathgart watched the whole operation with his hands on his belt. When the boat arrived, he faced Rascal Pratt. "Well," he said, "you'll be all right with these men. They seem upright enough. Not ones to mistreat a prisoner."

This is not exactly how Emma would have described the two sailors, each of whom looked about as untrustworthy as one can look and still manage to be employed. In fact, it was something of a puzzle to her that they could be employed by anyone at all, let alone by the same agency as her own father. But both Sergeant Cathgart and Rascal Pratt seemed to be in strangely high spirits, so she said nothing.

The sailor who had walked them down from the tunnel helped his mate pull the rowboat up onto the beach. "Here's the prisoner," he said. "Skipper said to stuff— er, to *put* him in the sail locker for the time being."

"I'd be happy to," said the second crewman, and turning to Rascal Pratt, he said mockingly, "So you're the *pirate*, are ya?"

Rascal Pratt simply ignored the man. Sergeant Cathgart then held out his hand and repeated his farewell from before, again promising Rascal Pratt that the men on the cutter would treat him well. "Good luck to you," he said finally.

Rascal Pratt took the sergeant's hand in his two shackled ones, and with a sly smile he said, "Thank you, Sergeant. From the looks of things, I won't need too much of that!"

The sergeant then turned to leave. As he did, he noticed Emma standing behind him. "Well hello, Miss Green, did you come to say goodbye too?"

Emma blushed, but Rascal Pratt, who also seemed to

notice her for the first time, brightened and said, "Oh, Miss Green, I'm glad you came down. What good fortune – I have a favor to ask of you. I saved a few tokens from Achilles' box. I put them right over there. I thought it fitting that some of Drake's treasure stay buried, and I always intended that the four of us – you, Harris, Sue and I – would take it back out to the rock together, as a sort of tribute to all the years it was out there, undiscovered. I'm a little superstitious I guess. Alas, we won't have time, now will we? Anyway, since you and Harris are the only ones who know where we found it, would you take it back there for me?"

"I-I suppose," stammered Emma, not sure what to make of this request. "But, neither Harris nor I are much good on the water."

"But you are," protested Rascal Pratt cheerfully. Emma found his good spirits to be more suspicious than ever. And indeed, Rascal Pratt went cheerfully on. "It would mean a lot to me if you would agree to it. But, go on, take a look, there's a box right over there in the cypress grove."

Emma turned around to look. About twenty or so yards away, just off the beach, was a large rock under a cypress tree. The rock was about Emma's height. Just between the rock and the trunk of the tree sat a box made from a few slats of very weathered wood. Emma walked cautiously to it. She felt everyone's eyes upon her. She lifted the lid and looked inside, expecting to see at least a handful of the gold pieces they had found. But inside, on the floor of the box, were only three gold doubloons. She picked one up. By an unnatural coincidence, a sunbeam happened to pierce the fog at that moment and the coin, in spite of its age, glowed a soft yellow. Emma turned it over in her hand and said, "But—."

She had intended to say, "But there are only three pieces

here." However before she could, Rascal Pratt cut in.

"Oh, yes," he said, "I know, it's a lot. Maybe too much. But I won't be needing it anymore. You're welcome to help yourself to some. Still, if it isn't too much trouble, please take the rest back to the place we found it."

Emma blinked at him in a state of befuddlement. And then, something clicked in her head, and she caught on. "Oh!" she said. "Oh yes – certainly." She threw the coin back into box, taking care that it should hit one of the two others and make a loud *clink*. "I'd be honored to take it back. Only, it's so *much* gold. It must be more than a sailor – such as yourself – could make in a year! Are you sure you can't keep it? Not *any* of it?"

Rascal Pratt held up the chains on his manacled hands and laughed. "No, it's better that it go back to the sea. Who knows, maybe someone else as old as Achilles has heard the tale and knows where to send his granddaughter to find it." He smiled with an exaggerated sadness, and Emma nodded sadly back, as if it were all part of a long and poignant tale.

Rascal Pratt turned suddenly to the sailor. "Well, sir, I'm ready," he said. He lowered his head humbly and held out his wrists. "Your prisoner."

The sailor didn't move. He looked from Rascal Pratt to the box beside the rock and back to Rascal Pratt with a suspicious glint in his eye.

Sergeant Cathgart, who had been standing by, watching all the while, cleared his throat. "Sailor, you know your duty. Take the prisoner to the ship." The other sailor, the one who had escorted them down from the tunnel was also still standing there. He moved to help his crewmate get Rascal Pratt into the rowboat. But Sergeant Cathgart said, "Sailor – what? Are you still here? Get back to your lieutenant and help him unload that powder! I don't want any more delays. I've a long walk to Sausalito now, no thanks to your skipper. I'll file a report about this and I'll be doubly angry if I make it back to San Francisco under my own steam and find I still have to wait for you. Now get going. Wait! Let's go together, I've a final piece of my mind I want to give to your Lieutenant What's-his-name before I start out on foot." With that, he nodded one last time to Rascal Pratt and Emma, took the first sailor by the shoulder, and marched him back up the trail, away from the cove.

Emma and Rascal Pratt watched them until they disappeared. Then Rascal Pratt turned to Emma again, but this time with a strange seriousness that took Emma by surprise. Letting out a long breath, he said, "Well, goodbye Emma Green. This really is goodbye, you know."

Now, just moments before, Emma had thought she understood Rascal Pratt's plan to escape. Therefore, she expected to see him again – presuming even that she would help him as soon as he tricked his captors and got back to shore. But this good-bye, this very sincere good-bye, this perhaps most sincere good-bye she had ever received in her whole life, threw her, as it seemed certain that Rascal Pratt was no longer acting and really did mean not to see her again.

"But..." she said, wrinkling her brow and casting a glance in the direction of the cypress tree and the box containing the doubloons. Rascal Pratt cut her off, though, with a hard stare. And she quickly said, "Y-Yes, of course, I know."

"Courage, Emma," said Rascal Pratt. It was an odd voice, much older than usual, and warm in its way, though free of both unhappiness and cheer alike. "Our paths may yet cross again, sometime in the future, and in far different circumstances I hope. Until then, fare thee well." He bowed slightly.

There was little Emma could think of to say in return. Besides, she had lost her confidence and was almost too afraid to speak, as she might give something away. She did her best to smile and put on as courageous a face as she could.

That, apparently, was all Rascal Pratt needed. He smiled gently himself, then turned and stepped into the back of the waiting rowboat, taking special care, it seemed to Emma, not to look at her again.

The Mystery of Rascal Pratt

- 15 -
The Cutter

The sailor pushed the rowboat off the beach. Though Emma was standing on shore, she could hear him mutter as he rowed.

"My brother was killed in the war. Battle of the Wilderness. He didn't run."

And Emma heard Rascal Pratt's answer. "Battle of the Wilderness, you say? I'm sorry to hear that. I was there, you know. One of my brothers was killed there too." He went on talking, but a great gust of wind rolled through the cove, and Emma could hear no more.

She watched the rowboat until it reached the side of the cutter. She wanted to look away, as she couldn't bear to watch Rascal Pratt hoisted by his chained arms. But the sailor seemed to be in a great hurry, and even though he did haul Rascal Pratt roughly out of the rowboat and onto the cutter, he reappeared on deck so quickly again after taking her friend below – just moments later, really – that Emma was relieved. The sailor, bully though he certainly was, could not have made too much trouble for his captive in so short a time. And when he started to get back into the rowboat, Emma knew for certain that he had fallen for Rascal Pratt's ruse.

Emma quickly ducked into the boughs of a myrtle tree on the highest part of the beach, not far from the place where the trail up to the lighthouse began. Whatever Rascal Pratt planned to do, she hoped he would do it soon. She watched carefully for some movement on the boat, something to indicate he had gotten himself free. She waited and waited, but on the cutter, she saw nothing.

In the meantime, the sailor continued rowing for the beach. Just as it had been on its previous trip to shore, the boat was pushed sideways by the current, so the sailor had to row nearly double the real distance from the boat to the beach, much of it against the current.

As Emma watched, she heard someone coming down the trail. She supposed it to be more of the crew of the cutter, and she hid herself more deeply in the myrtle. She couldn't see the trail from where she was, but after a few seconds of listening, she realized that the footsteps she heard were much lighter and quicker than a grown sailor's heavy tread. She parted the branches of her hiding place, and to her surprise, she saw

Harris Cole standing at the end of the trail with his hands on his hips, looking out at the cove.

"Harris!" she called in a loud whisper, "Harris! Over here!"

Harris turned and looked around. It took a few seconds but eventually he saw Emma waving to him from her hiding place. With a puzzled look he crept into the thick boughs of the myrtle to join her and said, "Emma, what are you doing?"

"It's hard to explain. What are you doing? And how are you?"

"Well, I sure caught it from my dad, if that's what you mean," said Harris, rubbing the seat of his pants. "But I'm fine, more or less. I came to say goodbye to Rascal Pratt. Has he left already?"

"Yes," said Emma, "he's already aboard the cutter. They locked him in a sail locker I think – and he's in chains. He's a prisoner! They're taking him back to the Presidio, but they can't leave till the tide starts coming back in." And then, she told him how she thought Rascal Pratt was planning an escape. She told him of the scheme of the empty box of gold. She pointed to the rowboat and the sailor. By then, the sailor in the rowboat was very close to shore. "But whatever Rascal Pratt's planning, he better hurry," Emma said, now in a whisper, "the sailor is almost here."

"Maybe Rascal Pratt needs help." said Harris. "Maybe he can't get out of the sail locker." And then, determinedly, he added, "One of us should go out there."

"To the cutter?" demanded Emma with alarm. "We'd get caught for sure."

"One of us has to go out there," Harris insisted. "Even if Rascal Pratt does get out of his chains and out of the sail locker, he still can't sail the cutter by himself. He needs help."

"What do you mean, sail the cutter?" said Emma. "Why would he want to sail the cutter?"

"Well, he has to escape by sea, doesn't he? It's the only chance he's got. He can't come back to the cove, or they'll catch him for sure, especially with that leg of his. He's got to take the cutter. That's his plan, I'll bet."

"But…" Emma protested. The idea was so outlandish it had never occurred to her. If that was the plan, it was sure to end in failure. Emma's mind raced as she tried to think of another way, another means of escape. What they needed was another boat, something other than the cutter. Suddenly, she had an idea. "What about Achilles' boat? The reed boat? It's still on the beach! It's just on the far side of the cove."

"Of course!" whispered Harris excitedly, with a snap of his fingers. "We can take it to him." But then he stopped, and looking at Emma he said sadly, "Only, one of us has to stay here too. Someone has to give a signal if the sailor starts to row back out to the cutter."

"Oh, I can do that," Emma volunteered without hesitation, relieved to discover a role that involved staying on land. "Only, what should I do? Hoot… like an owl?"

"An owl, in the daytime?" said Harris hurriedly, as he crept out of the hiding place, on the far side of the tree from the beach and the sailor. "Well, all right, I guess that will do. But Emma, be careful. I wouldn't want to be standing around here when that sailor finds out there's no gold in the box."

"Oh, I'll be fine," said Emma. The sailor was a danger she would much prefer over going out on the cove, in a boat, in the fog. "But, we've got to hurry. Once you get to Achilles' boat, look back over here. I'll wave when the coast is clear.

You can paddle out and pick up Rascal Pratt. Say – maybe then the two of you can let the current take you around the point – you can't paddle against it anyway. But stay close to the cliffs this time. You don't want to end up in the Potato Patch again, especially in the fog."

Emma was proud of herself for these practical details, and Harris agreed. Emma then concealed herself back in her myrtle tree, and Harris retraced his steps up the trail a little way before making for Achilles' boat, which was a hundred yards or so to the east. Emma watched him as he went, ducking behind boulders and cypress trees and whatever other cover he came across. In the fog drifting into the cove more thickly than ever, he was almost invisible.

The sailor, meanwhile, had just stepped out of the rowboat and turned to pull it up onto the beach. Now was the time for Harris to make his move. When the sailor's back was to her, Emma waved. She wasn't at all certain Harris could see her, but after a short time she watched the dark outline of the little reed boat flop down into the shallow water of the far side of the cove. She saw Harris, who was scarcely more than a shadow, hop aboard. With just a few strokes of the paddle, he bore down on the cutter more quickly than he ever could have paddled the distance over still water – the strong ebb tide was with him and pulled him the entire way. Then he and the reed boat disappeared from view on the far side of the cutter, and moments later, Emma saw a head rise above the level of the deck, and next she saw a figure clamber aboard. The figure hesitated for a moment before disappearing down into the hatch.

Emma turned her attention back to the sailor. He was a wiry fellow, though with a belly that was surprisingly large for his otherwise thin self, and he seemed by nature quite suspicious. He had already beached the rowboat, though he didn't pull it up very high from the waterline – perhaps because he knew the tide was still falling. He checked around in all directions, then scuttled down the beach toward the place Rascal Pratt had left the box containing the doubloons.

Emma looked back out to the cutter. There was no sign that anyone had come back on deck yet. On shore, meanwhile, the sailor had just reached the little cypress grove. He located the box between the rock and the tree. He lifted it. It must have been unexpectedly light, for a worried expression suddenly clouded his face. He opened the lid. For a moment he was perfectly still. He slowly dumped the contents into his hand, staring at the three doubloons in obvious disbelief. Then, with a terrifying jerk, he lifted the box high above his head and smashed it violently to the ground – and even began to kick the pieces it broke into.

Emma hid herself deeper than ever and peeped anxiously through the boughs of the myrtle back out onto the cove, expecting, hoping, to see the little reed boat escaping from the cutter and making for the point, only with two figures on it this time instead of one. But this is not what she saw, not at all. Indeed, she could make out two figures, but they were still on the cutter – at least it seemed that Harris had succeeded in springing Rascal Pratt free. But they were not making any effort to get back into Achilles' boat. Rather, they had lifted it out of the water and were just then setting it on the deck of the cutter. As Emma tried to understand what this meant, she saw that now the figures on the deck appeared to be doing some sort of work, cranking a hand winch from the looks of it. And before long, a piece of canvas began to slide up the mast. They were hoisting a sail! But that wasn't part of the plan; at least, it wasn't part of Emma's plan.

So now it was clear: Rascal Pratt and Harris did intend to take the cutter. To Emma, this was terrible news, and she was certain that one day she would be visiting both of her friends in jail. Within a few seconds the sail was far enough up the mast that it began to snap in the breeze. Emma could hear it plainly and she waited for the sailor to realize what was happening and go charging back out to the cutter in his rowboat. But evidently he was still under the thrall of his own loss and was oblivious to all else around him, as he searched desperately among the rocks for the rest of his treasure. But Emma knew that sooner or later he would come to his senses and realize he had been duped. And then, no doubt, he would be crazed with anger and a desire for revenge, and he would be out to the cutter in a flash. She decided she must do something.

As quietly as she could, she stole out from her hiding place and crept down the beach to the rowboat. When she got there, she didn't know exactly what to do. Her first impulse was to smash a hole in the boat with a rock. But that was obviously a ridiculous idea, and she gave up on it almost as soon as she hatched it, as she felt certain the sailor would hear her and catch her in the act. Not only that, she wasn't actually sure she could do it. Looking more closely at the rowboat, she set her teeth and pondered. She noticed that the sailor, in his hurry, had not pushed it very high onto the beach. He had only thrown a few loops of line around a pole which Rascal Pratt had driven into the sand sometime before for the purpose of mooring his dory. It dawned on Emma that she might be able to push the sailor's rowboat off the beach and back out into the cove where, hopefully, the current would take it away. She wondered how heavy the boat was and if she could even push it at all. A little wave rolled up onto the rocky beach just then and floated the boat lightly off its bed of pebbles. The line between the boat and pole tugged taut, and as the wave subsided, it went slack again.

This gave Emma an idea. As fast as she could, she uncoiled the line from the mooring post and tossed it into the boat. She rested her shoulder against the boat's bow, and then waited. A few seconds later, another wave lifted the little vessel. Emma summoned all her strength and gave the rowboat a strong shove. Like magic, it was free. It floated backwards into the water, as light as a feather, then turned slowly, stern-end first, toward the point and the open sea. A satisfied thrill ran through her limbs and she might have lingered a moment longer to admire her handiwork except, just then and high over her head, she heard a familiar noise. It was a dog's bark. Emma recognized it at once. It belonged to Sammy.

She turned and looked. Sure enough, there was Sammy, on the path directly above her. He was looking down at her, poking his head through the rails of the fence where she had been not an hour before. And standing next to him, she could make out the figure of a man – her father. In the fog, it was difficult to tell if Captain Green had actually seen her, but her heart nearly stopped beating all the same. She had been so worried about the sailor from the cutter that it hadn't occurred to her she might get caught by her own father. Not knowing what else to do, she turned around quickly, pretending she hadn't seen him. She realized that he was more likely distracted by the goings-on out at the cutter, for the boys had succeeded in getting the anchor up, and Rascal Pratt was now at the larger boat's helm.

As Emma watched, the cutter's sail filled with air. It fell off the wind and began to make headway. The breeze and the ebb tide worked against each other and together they squeezed the cutter safely past the point of rock and out onto the bay.

In the meantime, the sailor's rowboat had drifted far down the shore and was drawing up to the huge boulders that marked the very end of the point. Emma knew that as far as the sailor was concerned, the rowboat was hopelessly lost. Assured of this, and mostly mindful of her father, she called out to the sailor in an innocent air, "Sir, your rowboat! It's drifting away!"

The Mystery of Rascal Pratt

- 16 -
Fog and Gun

The fog thickened by the moment. The breeze pushed scuds of froth onto the pebble beach. A small wave doused Emma's shoes and she took a step backwards onto the shore. She was watching the sailor in the little cypress grove who finally seemed to understand what had happened. She tried to guess what he would do if he suspected her. He was running just then toward the spot where Emma stood, while she feigned a concerned expression and pointed helpfully to the rowboat as it drifted away. The sailor panted from the effort of running across sand, though when he reached Emma, she saw that his face was filled with great rage.

At the same time, from the trail that led down to the cove, came the sound of footsteps making great haste. The sailor turned just in time to see Captain Green appear on the beach too. The wrath in the sailor's face dissolved instantly and was replaced by a look of panic. He looked out to sea at the escaping cutter and down the cove, at his lost rowboat. He looked at Emma, and then at Captain Green. Finally he looked at the three coins in his hand.

"But I... I..." he stammered, pointing wildly between the place his treasure was supposed to have been and the place the cutter actually was.

"Save it," growled Captain Green. "I expect your lieutenant will want to know. You'll find him up at the light. Maybe he's already seen what's happened."

The sailor didn't move. He stood staring dumbly at Captain Green.

"I wouldn't want to be in your shoes either," said the captain, "but I'd hurry all the same if I were you."

The sailor turned once more to gaze out on the cove, as if he held out hope that things could somehow change back to his favor. Then he shut his mouth, doffed his cap, and began to run up the path toward the lighthouse.

Captain Green waited until he disappeared, then turned to his daughter. Emma suddenly felt that she was now in the same position the sailor had just been, and she too opened her mouth futilely to explain how she happened to be down at the cove. But Captain Green cut her off with his raised hand and said, "Come along, young lady, this isn't over yet, you know."

Emma had to trot to keep up. They climbed the trail to the main path together, then hurried through the tunnel, their footsteps echoing sharply off the walls. When they came into the open again, Emma normally would have had a tremendous view of San Francisco Bay, the Golden Gate, and the Pacific Ocean. Now however, everything was obscured by fog, except the waters in the immediate vicinity of Point Bonita. Emma could still make out the cutter, but it was getting fainter by the second.

She noticed then that the boat's sails weren't full, and this confused her, as there could be little doubt that getting the cutter to disappear into the fog bank as soon as possible was Rascal Pratt's plan. At that very moment, she saw a figure on the boat run up to the bow. It was Harris, she felt certain, and he leaned over the rail with a long boat hook and deftly snagged something off the cutter's side. It was the very same rowboat that Emma had pushed into the current. A moment later the bow of the cutter fell a point or two to the lee, the sails again filled with wind, and the cutter began to track crabwise out the mouth of the bay once more, pulled by the current, and pushed abeam and away from the rocks by the cold northwest wind, the rowboat now tethered to its stern and tagging along obediently behind.

At the same time, there was much frantic activity at the lighthouse, and Emma could see this too from where she stood. She and her father had not yet crossed the bridge, and Sammy, who until then had run ahead of them, now waited just this side of it, whining and whimpering but not going any farther. Emma couldn't whine and whimper, but she had an awful pit in her stomach. She was terrified nearly out of her

skin for what was to come – as well as left feeling utterly pow-
erless now that it was all unfolding so quickly. Irrationally,
as though it might somehow halt time, she stooped to pat
her dog. But Captain Green crossed the bridge without hesitation, and it bounced under his step as he barked over his
shoulder, "Emma! Keep up!"

So Emma crossed too, and when she reached the stone
platform at the foot of the lighttower, she saw to her horror
that Lieutenant Walker's men were now setting up the fog
cannon, clearly with the intent to fire on Rascal Pratt and
Harris. Even Captain Green seemed surprised, and he said to
the lieutenant, "Good Lord, man, what are you doing?"

"What does it look like, John?" snapped Lieutenant
Walker, who was working feverishly.

"You'd fire on your own ship? But that's ridiculous!"

"I paid for that ship," said Lieutenant Walker curtly, "and
I can sink it. I'd rather sink it than know it's in the hands of
the enemy."

"Don't be so dramatic!" said Captain Green. "Your boat's
not in the hands of the enemy; it's in the hands of a boy. One
boy. And another he's taken prisoner." Here, Captain Green
looked sidelong at Emma, as though this were an important
distinction and something she'd do well to memorize. "And
if you ask me, we may yet get the cutter back."

But the younger officer ignored him and said impatiently,
"John, we're going to lose him in the fog. Do you want to help
or not?" And not waiting for an answer, he gave the order to
load the gun.

"No, I don't care to help!" cried Captain Green incredu-
lously. "Think about what you're doing – there's enough powder aboard her to blow a hole in the sky. Then you'll be in a
fine fix – you'll have lost a boat under your command. As

long as she's afloat, there's a chance you can recapture her."

"I can afford a new one," said Lieutenant Walker, and as he sighted out along the barrel of the cannon, he barked to his crew, "Ready to fire?"

"Richard, *think* about what you are doing," pleaded the captain. "At least one boy out there is completely innocent."

The lieutenant showed no sign of having heard Captain Green. He made a final adjustment to one of the screws that aimed the gun, and then said, "Steady, steady..."

"Stop!" commanded Captain Green. And to the men in the crew he shouted, "Listen to me, men, all of you, this is madness. Hold your—"

But just as he said this, the lieutenant dropped his hand and shouted, "*Fire!*"

Captain Green pulled Emma towards him by her arms. He swung quickly round in front of her and put his hands over her ears. There was a tremendous boom. Even with her father's hands over her ears and her head pressed into his stomach, Emma was still astonished by the sound. From that close distance it was many times louder than anything she could have expected, and the gun's muzzle lit the fog around them in a flash of brilliant orange. A cloud of white smoke and the sharp smell of sulfur engulfed the whole platform. A moment later, the smoke cleared and as it did, all eyes turned to the sea. Exactly at that instant, a plume of white appeared about fifty yards behind the cutter. They had missed. The lieutenant swore angrily and then cried, "Reload!"

Captain Green took the lieutenant by the shoulder. "Richard, hold your fire and I'll help you. I can help you save your command. Blame it on me if you like. But don't sink your own boat!"

"Save my command?" scoffed Lieutenant Walker, and he

turned to look at the captain as though he were some sort of simpleton. "I'm not going to lose my command. Don't you know who I am?" And then he turned back to his crew and shouted, "Prepare to fire!" He bent over the cannon, mumbling calculations to himself and making adjustments to the aiming screws. "Steady, steady, and... *fire!*"

This time, Emma clapped her own hands over her ears. There was another tremendous roar and another brilliant flash of orange. The cannon jumped back against the ropes the sailors had tied around its carriage. The air was again filled with smoke and the smell of sulfur. The smoke cleared and this time the white plume of water which showed where the cannon ball landed was much closer to the cutter, but still a few yards behind it.

Now it was Captain Green who swore. "Blast it!" he said, "If you're going to do it— " But just then he cut himself off and pulled out a little brass spyglass from inside his coat. He trained it on the cutter which now was hardly more than a ghost. Emma thought she saw a smile come to his lips. He folded the glass and returned it to his interior coat pocket. "If you are going to do it," he went on, "at least do it right. You're not putting in enough charge!" He shoved the younger officer aside and made his way through the crew toward the gun.

"Stand back!" bellowed Lieutenant Walker. "Stand back, *Lighthouse Keeper* Green, and remember your place!" And more quietly, to himself he added, "Mark my words, this last will do it."

"That's fortunate for you, as you've only time for one more shot, and it will be a long one," said Captain Green. "But your crew has no experience." Then looking from face to face of the men in Lieutenant Walker's squad, he barked, "Who here has seen action before?"

No one answered.

"Lubbers!" muttered Captain Green, almost as a curse. "Richard, I'm going to load the gun for you. Don't worry – you can take all the credit for the kill. I don't care about that. I've had my fill already." And without waiting for permission, Captain Green snatched one of the swabbing poles from a sailor and prepared to charge the gun. Emma was mortified that her father should help anyone so vile as Lieutenant Walker. Yet she was mesmerized by what she saw. Quickly and precisely her father plunged the swab down the barrel. He loaded the charge, ramming it into the gun with the charging pole. Finally, he picked up the last shot, the twenty-five pound ball of iron, lifted it to his chest, and carried it to the front of the gun.

"This is the important part," he said looking around as though to make sure everyone was watching.

"Spare me the lesson!" fumed Lieutenant Walker, "Just hurry, before we lose him in the fog!"

Captain Green shrugged. "Alright, but you must allow for the current. Notice how heavy the ebb is right now," he said.

Emma looked out to sea along with everyone else. She didn't take the time to gauge the speed of the outgoing tide. Instead she just thought, Hurry, Rascal Pratt. Hurry, Harris! Please *hurry*!

The lieutenant studied the cutter momentarily, then looked blankly back at Captain Green before shouting, "Just get OUT of the way!"

"Very well," said Captain Green with a heavy grunt. And giving a nod to the rest of the gun crew, he said, "You may fire when ready."

"I give that command!" the lieutenant cried, now nearly

beside himself in rage. He fiddled with the aiming screws one last time and shouted, "Now once and for all, stand clear!"

For every other shot, Emma's father had been at her side. But now he was trapped on the other side of the gun, and he stood back against the railing of the platform to get as far away from the muzzle of the cannon as he could.

Lieutenant Walker sited out once more along the barrel, whispering something inaudible to himself. Then, he gave the order. He didn't yell this time, but instead seemed to make a point to deliver the order calmly. "*Fire!*"

There was the briefest hesitation, after which it seemed as though things began to happen backwards. First, the gun carriage leapt violently against the ropes which restrained it. Next, came the shock of the report, which this time was much louder than before. And only then, or so it seemed, came the flash. It was orange, as before, though many times oranger, and it froze everything in its light, as though etching an image of all of them into the green and grey stone of the cliffs around the lighthouse.

The breeze cleared the smoke away. Everyone looked to sea. But the cutter was not there. It had completely disappeared. One of the men could be heard to ask under his breath, "Did we hit her?"

"Quiet!" the lieutenant growled, holding up his hand. The man shut up, and except for the breeze and the never-ending thump of the waves breaking below, all was quiet. The sea became just the sea again, and were it not for the score of anxious eyes peering into the fog from the parapet around the tower, the lighthouse would have been just a lonely outpost.

But then, deep, deep in the fog bank, there was a sudden and sickening flash of yellow. Something had exploded at sea. It exploded in a chain of violent spasms of yellow, white, and orange, and it lit up the fog bank in the same jagged and fitful way that lightening flashes through a cloud. A moment later, the sounds of explosions reached them — terrible, rolling booms, each louder than the previous. It seemed to go on forever, like the very last of a fireworks show. But eventually the flashes stopped, and the final echoes of thunder rolled out of the fog and across the bay. All was quiet again.

On the platform though, the quiet did not last long. After a brief delay, the sailors began to shout with joy, all at the same time. The sound of their happiness at such a thing made Emma ill. They clapped their lieutenant on the shoulder, congratulating him as a smug look of pleasure spread over his face and he allowed himself to become the center of their jostling. One or two of the men threw their hats in the air. Emma, whose face was now wet with tears, watched the caps sail upward. They were caught in the breeze and blown over the rail of the platform to fall into the sea behind Emma's father.

Her *father*. Emma narrowed her eyes and fixed on him a look of intense dislike. But oddly enough, Captain Green winked when he caught her gaze. It was as though he were inviting her into a grand, practical joke. And while everyone else, aside from him and his daughter, celebrated, Captain Green leaned over the railing and pushed something heavy away from him. The thing fell. Emma caught her breath when she saw what it was: it was the cannonball, the one that should have gone into that last, horrible shot. Her father must have hidden it somehow in his coat, and now he was disposing of it. It all happened so quickly that it took Emma a few moments to comprehend what had happened. At last she understood: on its last shot, the cannon had fired nothing but noise. She came to this realization as she watched the ball fall harmlessly over the railing and plunge toward the waves below.

Emma's legs failed her. She slumped back against the outside wall of the lighthouse and sank down onto the floor of the platform in a state of complete exhaustion while all around her, men whooped and cheered each other. Her father stepped across the platform to where Emma was and scooped her into his arms.

"Let's go," he said, "let's leave these men to their party. They deserve it – particularly seeing as how they now have a *very* long walk ahead of them."

He set her down on her feet and, hand-in-hand, they walked around to the landward side of the lighthouse and crossed the bridge, where they found Sammy waiting for them, cowering behind a rock.

"Come on, Sammy," said Captain Green. "It's over now. I'm tired of that sound myself." The three of them made their way along the path to the tunnel. It was only there that Captain Green permitted Emma to speak.

"B-But I don't understand," Emma stammered. "I mean, I know there was no ball in the last shot, but I saw the explosions out at sea!"

"That was the invention of your friend Rascal Pratt," said Captain Green with a chuckle. "He must have put several kegs of the powder in the rowboat and set it adrift. I suppose he set it off with a fuse."

"But how did you know he would do that?" said Emma.

"I didn't, that is, until I saw the boys through the spyglass. I saw them loading the barrels into the dinghy. And thank goodness, for that's what gave me the idea of meddling with the lieutenant's last shot. Now Emma, I also saw them lowering Achilles' boat over the side. If we hurry down to the cove, I have a feeling we'll see your friend Harris arriving in his little craft."

Emma's head was still swimming as she tried to put all the events in order, and she looked up with alarm at this last news. "But, Harris can't possibly paddle in from out there," she said. "We— I mean, *he* has tried it before."

"Ah ha," said the captain, raising a finger and opening the cover of his watch, "this time, he has no choice but to come in. He's coming in with the tide, you see. The tide has turned."

The Mystery of Rascal Pratt

- 17 -
Epilogue

*15th of September, 1866: The steam schooner, Dorado, and
two fishing yawls, all of San Francisco. The 4-master, Pegasus, of
New Bedford, a side-wheel bark, the Elliott Richie, of Cuba.*

Emma copied those words into her journal. She started
to add something, but stopped, and set both the book and
her pencil on the table in front of her. She was sitting that
morning in the lantern room. In the watch-room, on the level
below, the door to the outside of the lighthouse was open.

Emma took a deep breath. The air was perfumed by the tiny white blossoms of coyote brush that grew everywhere along the bluff, and warm drafts of it drifted in and out of the tower. She could tell it was going to be another fine, autumn day.

Three months of fog had come to a sudden end the week before, surprising everyone – some people still not believing it, and they warned that it would be back for a final hurrah. Still, whether summer would be back for one last round, or whether the autumn was here for good, the change was remarkable.

It was especially remarkable to Emma. She had never imagined something as soft and gray as fog could change the way she looked at the day – starting with getting out of bed and ending with things surprisingly far in the future, like her dreams of what she was going to do when she was grown, for example. In fact, she was not even aware it had done this, dulling everything a little bit everyday, until finally it actually went away, evaporating one night just before sunset, unveiling a sky that was crisp, fair, and full of possibility – and which must have been there all that time, just out of reach, and which now allowed the color to rush back into all of life, including her dreams.

She sat without moving, enjoying the peacefulness of the room. After a while – and Emma didn't know how long – her dog Sammy, who was by now almost full grown, sat up at her feet and scratched behind his ear, jangling his collar. Emma stirred, as if she had awakened from a pleasant dream. Time to get to work, she thought, time to work on my *project*.

She turned to get her schoolbooks, and as she did, she saw her journal, still open, sitting in front of her. She moved to close it but stopped and re-read the entry she had just copied from the lighthouse log. Once more, she started to put the journal away but again hesitated, this time chewing her pencil for a second or two in contemplation before finally giving in to the urge to write something more.

I really have to get going on my homework, before Mother sees how little I have done. So I'll try to be brief: I just realized that I forgot to mention the GOOD NEWS that we worked out. As you may have guessed, the good news is I don't have to leave Point Bonita. But I promised Mama I would keep up my studies. Papa's going to teach me math and science, and Mama is going to teach me literature and languages, and also music, because she thinks music is good for the brain. The promise I made to her though is that I would work on a 'project document.' I would write everything I learn, see, and observe in a 'document' while out here at Point Bonita. If you ask me, a project document is really just another (and not very pretty!) word for 'journal', one with lots of little notes about whatever I come across. But Mama says writing in my journal is different from "documenting" life out here at Point Bonita. Anyway, she read about project documents in a magazine she started having sent to her called "Modern Pedagogy." Pedagogy is Greek, by the way, for 'teaching'. And Mama is a pedagogue – that's a teacher, which reminds me: I also forgot to say that Mother accepted the job as the schoolteacher in Sausalito. Papa thinks it's a complicated arrangement, but I don't think it's so bad, at least for me. I only have to go to Sausalito on Wednesdays. Of course, I have to go on Fridays too to help Mama get ready to come back to the Point for the weekend. And then there are two Thursdays a month when I actually have to stay the night in Sausalito because, well just because, and also the third Tuesday, I think, of each month because of something about one of the social clubs in town which we promised could borrow the don-

key cart. Harris is going to help me get back and forth and help Mama too, though she will stay in Sausalito every other night during the week in the room above the schoolhouse. So you see, it's not really as complicated as Papa lets on, and it will be much easier going back and forth now with the donkey cart – it actually fits on the silly path, not like the huge wagon that takes a real mule to pull. But anyway, the important part is I can stay(!) at Point Bonita and help Papa with the light, and, oh yes, did I mention we bought the donkey cart? We bought it from Mr. Cole, Harris's father. Poor Harris.

Emma was just going to start another paragraph when she was interrupted by a sound from outside, the click, click, click of footsteps coming across the bridge.

Sammy heard it too and stood and barked his sharp little bark. The footsteps grew louder and with them came Emma's mother's voice. "Emma? Where are you, dear? I have something for you."

"I'm up here, Mama!"

Mrs. Green came into the lighthouse and stood in the watch-room with her hands on her hips, peering up the ladder at Emma. "Are you really trying to do your school work up there? Why don't you do it down here at the table? Wouldn't that be more comfortable?"

"Oh, I don't know," said Emma absently, still thinking about what she wanted to write. "I like the light up here better."

Her mother sighed and started to climb the ladder. At this, Emma roused herself from her thoughts and in a panic looked about for her schoolbooks, especially for her project, as her mother called it. Only then did she remember she had left those books downstairs.

Mrs. Green reached the top of the ladder. Sammy greeted her with a lick on her face as she emerged from the hole in the floor, and she had to push him away to step off the last rung of the ladder and up into the lantern room. "Emma," she said as she wiped her face, "isn't it dangerous to climb the ladder with Sammy?" But then she stopped herself and laughed. Emma was leaning comically over the desk, trying to obscure her journal from her mother's view.

"Tisk, tisk," said Mrs. Green with a chuckle, "I see you're not working on your project at all, you're writing in your diary."

"My *journal*," said Emma.

Mrs. Green smiled, "Sorry, dear, of course, your journal. Anyway, you aren't actually doing schoolwork. Such a tragic fate for you – daughter of the schoolteacher!"

Emma laughed. "Oh, Mother, it's not so bad!"

"Well, that's good, I'm glad to hear it. Anyway, I have a letter for you. I picked it up yesterday in town." And from a pocket in the front of her dress, Mrs. Green produced an envelope.

"A letter?" said Emma. "From who?"

"From *whom*?" corrected her mother, "Well, I believe it's from Sue."

"From *Suem*?" said Emma. They both laughed.

Emma took the letter from her mother. She started to open it, but stopped and looked at Mrs. Green suspiciously.

Mrs. Green laughed again and said, "My goodness, do you suppose I'm really going to try to peak at your letter?"

"Oh – no, of course not," said Emma, blushing and wondering herself at her secretiveness. All the same, she turned a little away from her mother and finished opening the envelope, holding it very close to her chest as she did.

Mrs. Green patted Emma on the head. "Don't worry, honey, I'll leave you alone to your plotting."

Emma looked up at her mother sheepishly and smiled and said, "Oh Mama, I just..."

"I know, I know – schoolteacher, mother – you know, even I sometimes find myself to be entirely untrustworthy! But have no fear, I must go back to the house, perhaps to pester your father. Enjoy your letter, but then get back to your project. You know, today you could write the notation about the seals. Haven't you been meaning to? That seems the most obvious one to me. They're called pinnipeds, you know, and there are three species here, Steller's Sea Lion—"

"Mother," moaned Emma, who at that moment was interested only in the letter.

"All right, all right, I'm leaving," said Mrs. Green, holding up both hands. "But don't forget – schoolwork!"

Emma smiled and shook her head as her mother made her way down the ladder. When she heard Mrs. Green's footsteps on the bridge again, she turned her attention back to the envelope. She finished opening it, took the letter out, and unfolded it. It was written on a delicate piece of onionskin paper, with a fountain pen. Sue had obviously been practicing her handwriting, as it was beautiful and flowing. Emma turned it over, looking at it enviously. Then she turned it back to the front and began to read.

Dear Emma,

Harris Cole came to visit yesterday. I'm sure you know this, since he accompanied your mother when she came to San Francisco to buy materials for school. Now, I do hope you are applying yourself on your project – Mrs. Green is very enthusiastic about it. She says it's the modern way to teach young people, the way of the future. I'm glad I'm not doing a project myself, but do let me know how it goes.

Speaking of school, I'm auditioning at the San Francisco School of Opera this week. Does that come as a surprise? I went to one, an opera, and I've caught the bug! It's beautiful. Come visit and we'll go see one. I've been practicing with a private teacher for almost a month now, a nice lady from Sicily who lives down the street, and my audition is in a few days. Wish me luck!

But, anyway, back to Harris. We had a lovely time, it was wonderful to see him. He caught me up on many things, including the rest of your exploits this summer. Goodness, how exciting! I'm just sorry I missed it!

Emma put the letter down for a moment and looked out the window. Both she and Harris had written to Sue several times since Sue moved away and had alluded to Rascal Pratt's escape. But neither of them had dared to put anything on paper about their own roles in it. That was their secret. Theirs, and Captain Green's, of course. Emma, however, knew that on this trip, Harris had intended to fill in Sue on *all* the details. Emma picked up the letter again, and rereading the last paragraph, she could see that Harris had done just that. So, at last Sue had the real story of the Battle of the Potato Patch, as the newspapers called it, though the newspapers had written a decidedly different version than the one Emma and Harris, and now Sue, knew to be true. Emma smiled and read on.

You know, I tried my best to let Harris know that he certainly has nothing to feel bad about, neither on my account nor Achilles'. And to tell you the truth, I think he believes me. Certainly, he was embarrassed when I first opened the door. I could see it in his eyes – or couldn't rather, since he wouldn't look at me directly. But he got over it quickly and spent a long time here with us, and especially with Achilles. They sat in the garden for hours talking about old times. Achilles thinks of Harris as a son. And also I know that for Achilles one of the saddest things about the whole affair is that he actually used to think that way of Mr. Cole too. But here is something that alarms me: I understand Achilles plans to visit Mr. Cole. He says there is a lake on the mountain beyond the rancho, where he used to take Mr. Cole as boy, and he wants to go there with him one last time. I'm writing to you because I'm a little bit afraid. Achilles is old, as you know. And he is now completely blind. If they do go up to that lake, he will have to rely on Mr. Cole for a lot. One thing Achilles is absolutely dead set on is that he wants to go with Mr. Cole alone. He doesn't even want Harris to go. I think Achilles will wait for a while, maybe another month or so, but still, do you think I'm worrying about nothing? You're at the Coles' a lot these days, and I would be very keen to hear what you think. Maybe I can ask your mother and father too. I owe you all a visit anyway.

When Emma read this, she put the letter down again to wipe her eye. She always had cried easily. Harris and Sue made fun of her for this. But it was all just too heartbreaking. It was, what was the word, it was *tragic*. As Sue said, Emma had actually visited the rancho quite a bit of recent, especially since Harris went back and forth to Sausalito with her and attended school there some days too. Emma knew that life at the Coles' had indeed become very unhappy.

A shadow had fallen over the rancho, and unlike the rest of the valley, it didn't leave with the sparkling arrival of autumn. All the gold Achilles and Rascal Pratt had given Mr.

Cole, which should have made his life easier, actually seemed to make it harder and seemed to gall him every time he spent it. But spend it he did, and on the strangest things – horses he couldn't afford to keep, card games, and especially on whiskey. Whiskey, whiskey, whiskey – the house was full of it. Harris even said the money was a curse and he couldn't wait for the day when it was all gone.

But hardest of all for Emma to see was the way Mr. Cole treated his son. He seemed to think Harris was in league against him, with the workers on the rancho, with the neighbors, with Emma even. He constantly reminded his son who was the father, who was the boss, and who had taught whom his so-called values. He treated Harris poorly, even though it was clear he was ashamed of himself for doing it. Yet Emma never heard Harris complain. One day though he had told her that he had decided to seek Achilles' advice; if there was one person who could help him save Mr. Cole from himself, it was Achilles. And now, from the sound of it, Achilles was planning a trip back to the rancho, back *home* – as it was known Achilles still called it, in spite of everything.

Emma sighed. She didn't look forward to a big confrontation between Mr. Cole and Achilles. She was afraid for Harris too. At least it sounded like the visit was still a month or two away. She hoped Achilles and Harris knew what they were doing.

Emma looked down at the letter one last time. There was just a little more.

Anyway, Emma, thanks for your help with this – and with everything. I know some people would call it superstitious to say you are good luck, but I don't, I just say thanks where it's due. I really hope to see you soon. You know, I love it here in San

Francisco. I like living in the city, and I love our little house on Russian Hill, probably like you love living out there on the Point. But I miss you, I miss Harris, and I miss our days at the cove.

Just one more thing – I saw the strangest newspaper article the other day. I think it will interest you greatly. If I can find it, I'll enclose it with this letter. Let me know what you think. If it's true, I say it's simply grand!

Your friend,
Sue

Emma flipped back through the sheets of paper the letter was written on. She didn't find anything folded inside them. She looked on the desk and even on the floor, but saw nothing else, and was just about to decide that Sue hadn't found the newspaper article after all when she picked up the envelope and shook it one last time. Something small fell out and fluttered down to the floor. It was a scrap of newspaper. As Emma watched it fall, she felt something flutter in her stomach too. She hesitated, for a reason she didn't really understand, then picked up the paper, squinted, and read aloud:

"Sydney, Australia – Commandant Edward Fisher of the Ministry of Gaols and Prisons was relieved of his post following the daring escape of a convict from the prison colony in Hobart, Tasmania. A small sailing vessel, which at least one witness said was armed with a single, modern cannon, but flew no insignia, is said to have entered the harbour just before sunset and shot a hole through the outer wall of the prison. Several convicts escaped. With the exception of one, all are reported to have been captured. Authorities are still searching for one prisoner remaining at large and also for the sailing vessel."

Emma lowered the scrap of newsprint. Her hands trembled. She set the clipping cautiously on the table, almost as though she didn't quite think it safe, even though it was very small. Her thoughts raced. She tried to estimate how long it would take a small boat to reach Australia – if it could at all – and how long it would take the news to return to San Francisco. She bent over the clipping again without daring to touch it, and re-read the place-names: Sydney, Hobart, *Tasmania*. She thought of her poor friend, Rascal Pratt, so far away. Even the sound of those names was remote and lonely.

Emma looked out from the light tower. The earth spread below her, a great disc of ocean and rock. She heard the calls of seabirds and the bark of seals – the sounds of her home. Then, a certain thought came to her, and she said aloud the names of *this* place, her own place. *California, San Francisco, Point Bonita*. And as she pronounced each of these names, she wondered what the people of Sydney, of Hobart, of Australia thought of them. She wondered about her friend Rascal Pratt. For all she knew, he was happy and free somewhere across the wide reaches of the southern sea. And looking down from her tower, she smiled, as it occurred to her that maybe it was he who, half way around the globe, thought Point Bonita the very ends of the earth.